TILL THE CAT LADY SINGS

ELLEN RIGGS

Till the Cat Lady Sings

Copyright © 2020 Ellen Riggs

ISBN 978-1-989303-59-7 eBook
ISBN 978-1-989303-58-0 Book
ASIN B088DHL25C Kindle
ASIN 1989303587 Paperback
Publisher: Ellen Riggs

www.ellenriggs.com
Cover designer: Lou Harper
Editor: Serena Clarke
2010061144

CHAPTER ONE

K eats and I sat side by side on the porch swing to enjoy the rare luxury of simply staring out at the big red barn and wide pastures dotted with livestock. I pushed off and swung back, off and back, mesmerized by both the movement and the beauty of it all. The magic hour right before sunset added a warm golden glow that would make any scene breathtaking, but this view was special because it was all mine.

"Isn't it amazing?" I said. Since much of the outdoor work was all mine, too, I had few opportunities to sit and appreciate how blessed I was to be here. But tonight, forced to wait for my best friend, Jilly Blackmore, to finish dressing for a party—something that had taken me 10 minutes, shower included—I basked in the utter serenity of Runaway Farm.

There was a grumble beside me and I glanced down. Keats, my black-and-white border collie with one blue eye and one brown, had taken far longer to prepare than Jilly and I put together. It had been a 10-minute fight just to get him into the bathtub. The bravest dog I'd ever known was terrified of water—even more so since our recent tangle with a colony of feral cats in Huckleberry Marsh. But there was no way he could go to this party stinking of farm. My mom was more daunting than a squirming sheepdog and getting Keats past her into the event was going to be a tough sell as it was. I was determined to try, because crowds made me anxious and I needed my unofficial therapy dog for moral support.

"What?" I said, as he directed his eerie blue eye up at me. "Can't a hobby farmer and innkeeper take a moment to bask?"

He offered his signature mumble of protest deep in his throat. This dog wasn't bred for lounging in a porch swing, or anywhere else. He liked being busy. In fact, he craved work like I craved my morning coffee. No job was too big or too small... unless it involved water. Sitting up, he shook himself all over, as if throwing off the fresh smell of shampoo.

"I get it." I ran my hand over his sleek coat, a move that normally left a layer of grit on my fingers. "You're embarrassed about looking so good. Me too, actually. This dress feels like a costume and I miss my overalls. But you look very dapper, buddy. Your whites have never been whiter."

The look he gave me was the canine version of a scowl. Keats was happiest belly down in dust and manure as he kept tabs on his livestock.

"It's just for one night, and it's important to Mom," I said. "Launching her own business after losing so many jobs is a genius move. This time no one can fire her."

"Except for her daughter," Jilly said, as she stepped through the front door looking spectacular. When we lived in Boston, she dressed up every day, saying it was a key to her success as a corporate headhunter. Since her stilettos touched down in Clover Grove, however, there had been a gradual erosion of personal style until she was just a few rungs above overalls. I hadn't seen her curly blonde hair blown out in ages and was surprised to see how much it had grown in farm country. Meanwhile, her iridescent emerald dress made her green eyes pop and her heels were an accident waiting to happen.

My brother, Asher, a police officer that half the women in town coveted, already adored "casual Jilly." There'd be no hope for him after seeing "glamorous Jilly."

"I give it a week before Iris calls a family meeting and asks Daisy to boot Mom from the business."

Of my four sisters, Iris was the most reserved, and her desire to open a business in partnership with Mom had come as a shock. I had no doubt that Daisy, the eldest, and our unofficial matriarch, would be in constant demand to negotiate among warring parties.

Perching beside Keats on the swing, Jilly smoothed her dress. "You're right about a lot of things, Ivy, but you underestimate your mother. I've helped a ton of people find their true calling in life, and I really think this is Dahlia's. Look at how fast she made it happen. Robbi Ford gave up Crowning Glory less than two weeks ago."

"Gave up" was being kind. The longtime salon owner had no choice but to close after her unspeakable crimes took her out of commission. Mom and Iris swept in with backing from all of us, and a business start-up loan. I had a sneaking suspicion that their association with Kellan Harper, Chief of Police, made the bank more receptive to their pitch.

"They've turned that place around fast with help from a great team," I said. "Tonight's grand opening party wouldn't be happening without your organizational prowess."

She shrugged before wrapping a silvery cashmere pashmina around her bare shoulders. "That's *my* true calling, I guess. Planning and catering events. Luckily things have been quiet here at the inn."

"Quiet" was also being kind. My business was currently dead. "Dead" was unkind but nonetheless true. Runaway Farm had been marked by murder three times during my relatively short tenure. Three times, Keats, Jilly and I had helped solve those murders and vindicated the farm. But people only remembered the murders and not the skillful sleuthing. I couldn't really blame them. Who'd want to escape the city for a bucolic farm experience where murder was as common as cow flaps?

Keats gave a little whine and rested his long muzzle on my lap. My hand dropped to the soft fur between his ears. He rolled his sympathetic honey brown eye up at me, offering an instant infusion of comfort and confidence.

"Don't worry, Jilly," I said. "I'll drum up some guests for us soon. Maybe even tonight. I've got a pocketful of business cards that I intend to empty before the party ends."

"Good plan," she said. "All except the pocket. I hope you don't mind but I hung a different dress in your room. The one you're wearing looks a little too..."

"Sensible?" I said. My options were limited as I'd tossed nearly everything I owned after leaving my corporate human resources job at Flordale Corporation in Boston. There was just one charcoal wool suit I'd kept for funerals, never expecting it to see so much use.

"No offense, my friend, but you might as well borrow one of Edna Evans' ancient nursing uniforms. She's not using them right now."

That made me smile. After a recent brush with death, my crotchety neighbor had hopped on a long-haul flight to Australia to clean up some family business. She'd left her large colony of feral cats in my care, which was turning out to be a much bigger worry than I'd anticipated.

"I can't borrow your dress," I said. "I stained your second-favorite sweater with ketchup."

"Never mind that," she said. "It was a small price to pay to bring you and Kellan Harper back together."

I laughed. "Well, I imagine he would have gotten around to kissing me eventually. But the ketchup obviously served as an aphrodisiac."

"You've made a good start, but the way you keep interfering in his police cases is bound to slow your progress," she said. "The poor man is infatuated and infuriated in equal parts. Tonight you need a dress that will tip the balance. It's in your room now, along with the right shoes and clutch."

"If Kellan doesn't like me in my natural state, then—"

She cut me off with a flick of manicured fingertips. "I'll come at this another way. Your mom specifically said no dogs tonight, which is totally reasonable given potential clients could have allergies. I know Dahlia Galloway, and if you waltz in looking like a million bucks she might not even notice Keats."

Glaring at her, I got up off the swing. "Using my therapy dog against me isn't fair."

"I'm trying to make sure Keats is at your side, so that you two can mumble all night in your weird private language. Just try not to freak people out with that stuff."

I walked over to the door. "You talk to Keats too, in case you hadn't noticed."

She pushed back with one stiletto and let the swing go. "Don't think it doesn't worry me that the dog and I understand each other better every day. But unlike you, I know strangers find that unnerving. We need business, Ivy. So go doll yourself up."

When I came back, Jilly was standing on the front walk, bellowing for Keats.

"Oh no," I said, wobbling down the porch stairs in borrowed finery and heels a half size too large. "You didn't let him go."

"He didn't ask my permission."

She gestured to a tornado of dust travelling across the driveway toward the enclosure containing the alpaca, llamas and donkeys. I didn't need the cloud to dissipate to know what was inside. In moments, a ball of black, white and orange unfurled and a very fluffy marmalade cat leapt onto the fence just in time for Keats to charge directly into the post. He bounced back and sat down hard.

"Stop it," I shouted. "Keats, *come*. And Percy, you stand down. I know you started it."

"Percy?" Jilly asked. "He finally has a name?"

"It took me a while to believe he was staying," I said. The cat had been part of Edna's feral colony until recently. "Why would he want to give up his freedom to live with a cat-hating dog? When I took him in to get his shots I had to offer a name, and Percy Bysshe Shelley is what came out. He's a chatty poet like Keats."

She shook her head. "You call that yowling poetry?"

"I love all the sounds my animals make. The smells... not so much."

"Speaking of which, we'd better get going before the farm's bouquet permeates our clothes." Her nose wrinkled. "I often wonder how much we stink to others."

"Me too. Turning the manure as often as I do, I suspect two showers a day aren't enough."

Jilly clicked ahead of me over the flagstones toward the

big black pickup truck. "That's why I gave our dresses a little shot of perfume."

"Let's take Buttercup," I said, gesturing to the old yellow Volvo sedan parked further away. "It'll put both Mom and Kellan in a good mood."

Buttercup had been my mother's four-wheeled pet before Asher basically seized the car. A long string of traffic violations had made Mom a menace on the road and my brother a laughingstock among his colleagues. Recently, Kellan had asked me to drive Buttercup because my truck was winning the battle over the manual transmission. My frequent stalls around town worried Kellan, and possibly made him a laughingstock, too. Buttercup was hardly a sweet ride, since she predated power brakes and steering, but at least there was no clutch.

I opened the driver's door and turned, expecting Keats to be behind me, eager to get in. The only thing he liked as much as herding was car rides. Instead, the dog was making frantic leaps at the gate where the cat appeared to be pawing at the latch.

"Percy, no!" I dropped my purse in the car and started to run. It was too late. The gate swung open and Drama, the feistiest of the llamas, wasted no time lunging through it.

If the escapee were a lamb or a goat, Keats would have had the situation handled in under a minute. Drama Llama was an entirely different matter. Like all camelids, he came into the world wired to loathe dogs. Even Alvina, the sweet dancing alpaca, mistrusted Keats although she would never aim a kick at him. Drama Llama had been waiting for his chance to do just that and now the cat had offered up the dog on a silver platter.

Jilly screamed as the woolly white creature took off after Keats. I'd seen my dog move fast, but never as if the devil himself were on his tail. Even so, he managed to keep his sheepdog wits about him and lured the llama in a big circle around us. They disappeared behind the barn and I held my breath until they emerged on the far side. Drama was gaining on Keats and this would end badly if I didn't run interference. Literally.

Kicking off Jilly's heels, I raced toward them, somehow managing to intercept the llama just moments before he reached the dog. Drama slammed on his cloven brakes and skidded but it was too late. He collided with me so hard that I fell flat on my back. The next few minutes compressed like a fan in my mind as I stared up at the sunset sky. A green blur passed and a latch clicked.

Keats licked my forehead until Jilly swam into focus and offered her hand. "You okay?"

"I think so," I said, sitting up. "You got him?"

"Keats lured the llama inside and circled back like a fireball so I could slam the gate." She looked over at the pen. "Drama is shredding my pashmina with his hoof right now. Maybe it's a statement about shearing."

"Where's the cat?" My voice sounded ominous, even to me. "He is so fired. There's only one thing on his job description: ridding the barn of vermin. And yet the mice frolic while he's out here unleashing dangerous animals."

Jilly pulled tissues out of her purse and tried to brush off my dress. *Her* dress. It had been such a pretty pink before its collapse.

"Percy was just doing what cats do," she said. "They're brats. You can't fire him."

I shook myself just as Keats had earlier. "They didn't call me the grim reaper of HR for nothing, my friend. I will downsize that cat's fluffy butt without a moment's regret.

When Edna gets back, I will hand him over in a carrier with a black bow on the handle."

She trailed after me to the car, clucking like a fussy hen. "Ivy, you need to go back inside and shower. Your feet are filthy."

I slipped behind Buttercup's wheel. "The ball's over for this Cinderella," I said, accepting the sandals she passed me. "What would a farmer do with glass slippers, anyway?"

CHAPTER TWO

I glared at the dog over my shoulder as I drove the big yellow sedan slowly down the twisty lane. Buttercup didn't like pressure. Too much pedal to the metal caused a vibration and then a squealing sound. With a little coaxing and finesse, however, she'd move along as nicely as my old mare, Florence.

"Honestly, Keats." I glanced over my shoulder at him and then shook my head. His white bib was now decidedly gray. "Quit letting that cat get to you. You're way too smart to fall for Percy's tricks. It's like something trips in your brain."

Keats mumbled something that sounded like an embarrassed apology.

"Go easy on him," Jilly said. "This has been a big adjustment. I think his feelings are hurt over how much time you're spending with Percy."

The whine from behind us was a little overdone. Then Keats pawed at the back of the passenger seat a few times, hard enough to leave marks on the brittle tan leather.

"Stop that," I told him. "You know how Mom feels

about Buttercup's upholstery." He whined again. "What is with you?"

"I told you, he's hurt," Jilly said. "He's a mama's boy."

I laughed. "Well, he'll always be my favorite, no question. This week I just had a couple of appointments to get Percy properly vetted after life in the wilds. I couldn't bring Keats because the cat was like a crazed cougar in the crate." I held out my arm to reveal a trio of nasty scratches. "So far, he's more trouble than he's worth."

Now the soundtrack from Keats sounded more positive, as if he hoped Percy would be sent packing.

"All I'm saying is that you and that dog have a very special bond," Jilly said. "There's the upside, like when he's saving your life. And then there's the downside, when he's a little jealous and acting out. On top of everything, you gave him a bath."

I sighed and glanced at Keats again. "Right. It's been an emotional week for you, buddy. How about we trap Percy inside tomorrow and walk over to Edna's? Just you and me?"

His tail lashed with what he'd normally consider unseemly enthusiasm, and he gave a little yip.

"I thought Keats unsettled the colony," Jilly said. "Cori told you to keep them stable and chill until the trapping and rehoming begins."

Cori Hudson was a dog trainer and rescue expert from Clover Grove's more prosperous neighbor, Dorset Hills, better known as Dog Town. In fact, she was part of a group known as the Rescue Mafia, and had been close friends with Hannah Pemberton, the heiress who previously owned Runaway Farm. After seeing coverage of my newsworthy rescue of Keats, Hannah had offered to sell me the farm for a deal I couldn't refuse, and then moved with her family to Europe. Over time, her friends had crept out of the woodwork, and they'd recently helped me considerably. But my close connections with the police department meant we had to keep our contact minimal. Kellan had already voiced concerns about the Rescue Mafia's tendencies to prioritize animal welfare over the law.

"I'm worried about the colony," I said, turning the yellow parade float onto the highway and accelerating gently as we headed to town. "I think some cats are missing."

"Missing! How can you tell? There's over forty of them and they go and come as they like."

"Normally it's the same team of familiar faces. Some are quite friendly and let me pat them. But yesterday I didn't see any of those cats. It's like ten disappeared overnight. I went over later for a second look and still nothing."

"Maybe they went back to the swamp." Jilly looked a little worried now, too, probably fearing I'd ask her to come along to explore. Huckleberry Marsh was a spooky spot that sucked you right off the logs into the silty water.

"That was my first thought, so I went down there with Percy yesterday. There wasn't a cat to be found." I pressed the pedal a trifle harder, risking Buttercup's umbrage. My mom's umbrage over my being late was becoming the bigger concern. "What if Edna comes home and none of her cats are left?"

"I'm no expert, but I would assume feral cats roam. With Edna gone, they're probably checking out their options for winter. They don't know we have a master plan that will have them all basking by a warm fire before Christmas."

"Maybe. I just have a funny feeling about it. Keats will let me know if anything suspicious is going on."

"I'll come too," Jilly said, proving yet again why she'd

been named best friend in college and continued to win the award year after year. "Another set of eyes might help. Besides, I want Edna's homecoming to be peaceful. She deserves that after all she's been through."

"Agreed. I hope she comes home with some of her old feistiness, though. She was entirely too nice before she left. It was unnerving."

"That was only because she wants to make sure her house and cats are cared for and that her gourmet meals will continue to appear like clockwork upon her return."

We both laughed, and Keats dared to slip one dusty paw through the seats to see if Jilly might be amenable to sharing her prime spot. She flicked it off her dress promptly, killing that hope.

My throat started to tighten as we got closer to town. Mom and I were like camelids and dogs, and tension magnified our differences. This was one of the biggest nights of her life and she was bound to be combustible, which meant I needed to stay super cool.

"Breathe," Jilly said, gesturing to her lower abdomen. "Count up to seven and back down."

"Usually it's only five," I said.

"Seven's right for tonight. Maybe nine. I'll have to read the room and get back to you."

Her warnings frequently saved me from actions I'd live to regret. Back in our corporate days I had more self control, but a serious concussion during Keats' rescue had left me with a few deficits. A few assets, too. Most days I considered myself well ahead, if not fully right in the head.

I'd expected to nab a spot for Buttercup on Main Street because stores closed early and there wasn't much of a nightlife in Clover Grove. There was no parking to be had, however, and the sidewalks were busy, too.

"There must be an event," I said, as we slowed outside the salon.

"Yeah, silly," Jilly said, laughing. "The opening of the salon."

"What? All this is for Bloomers?"

Saying the word out loud made me wince. Mom's family had a floral naming convention. My sisters were Daisy, Iris, Poppy, and Violet, and all of us shared the middle name Rose. The name Bloomers did double duty as a play on "late bloomers," since Mom and Iris were starting all over. But Mom also knew the cheeky name would amuse the male customers she hoped to attract. Unlike its predecessor, Bloomers was a unisex salon and Mom would be offering simple cuts for men and classic straightedge shaving. Apparently she'd learned barbershop basics from her dad as a child—something I didn't know despite revising her résumé countless times.

It turned out you were never too old to be surprised by your mother. Indeed, her late-blooming popularity among the men of Clover Grove, and indeed all of hill country, had been an even bigger surprise. She was the belle of the midlife ball, and now she had her own ballroom.

"Nine," Jilly said, jarring me out of my trance. "In for nine, out for nine. I don't need to read the room to know that."

"I'll be fine," I said. "We don't need to stay long."

"I do. I'm helping Mandy with catering, remember? But I can ask Asher to run me home if you need to escape earlier. Just try to work the room a little with those business cards. You have a mission, remember?"

"In for nine, out for nine," I said, piloting Buttercup into a large spot on a side street.

I let Keats out and stood with the door open for a

moment, dusting off the pink dress as best I could. My feet were grimy and no amount of dusting could fix that. Hopefully Mom would be fluttering around too much to look down.

After dragging things out as long as I could, I shut the door and the three of us walked back to Main Street. It felt like I shrank with every step as confidence leaked out of me. By the time we reached the salon, I'd be the shortest "Galloway Girl" instead of the tallest. On top of everything else, I was worried people would ask questions about the murders that I didn't want to think about, let alone answer.

"Good luck," Jilly said, squeezing my arm as we walked in the door. "You just need to—"

Someone whisked her away before the last word was out of her mouth, but no doubt it was a reminder to breathe.

"Darling!" My mother hadn't specified black tie on the invitation and as a result, she was the only woman in the room in a floor-length dress. It was slinky, strapless, and her signature shade of red. To give her credit, she could pull it off despite being just "five feet and a smidge." Her wardrobe consisted of secondhand finds, most of them cleverly tailored so as to be unrecognizable to their former owners. No doubt she'd dyed her satin pumps, too. With seven mouths to feed and no job continuity, she'd learned to be creative.

She hugged me a little harder than usual and gave me a sniff.

"What are you doing?" I asked, pushing her away.

"Farm," she whispered, casing me from head to toe. "You look like it and smell like it. Oh my sweet lord, Ivy Rose Galloway. Your feet! What happened?"

"There was an incident. Don't ask." I craned around the room. "What a wonderful turnout, Mom. I see Heddy and

Kaye Langman from the antiques store, and Dina Macintosh from the pet boutique. There's Teri Mason chatting to Mabel Halliday. It's a veritable who's who of Clover Grove."

The decoy didn't work. Still looking down, she said, "What is that thing doing here? I distinctly said no dogs."

"Keats isn't just a dog," I said, as his tail beat quickly and steadily. "He's an essential component of my mental health. Can we not argue tonight? It's a special occasion."

Keats never took Mom's slings and arrows personally. He knew her moods and he knew she liked him. What's more, he liked her. He wasn't a dog to splash his affection around but he had plenty to spare for Mom.

"Dahlia!" A tall man came up behind Mom. He had plenty of hair that seemed oddly dark given the lines on his face. "You look stunning."

His arrival distracted Mom in a way I never could. She introduced me quickly. "Ivy, this is Wayne Flagg. He's been kind enough to let me practice my shaving and clipping skills on him."

"Good news," he said. "A reporter from the Clover Grove Examiner just interviewed me and took my photo to run with their story."

Mom rarely flushed, but she did now. Her red lips pressed into a thin line and I knew she was uneasy about the direction the story would take. Like any small town newspaper, the Examiner was a mix of real news and thinly veiled gossip and speculation. Reading between the lines was half the fun... unless you were the subject of the story. Now there was way too much to say about us, what with Mom's colorful history and the recent murders associated with my farm.

"All publicity's good publicity," Iris said, hovering with

Daisy in a two-woman security detail designed to protect Bloomers' reputation from Mom's verbal indiscretions.

All five Galloway Girls took after our mother, with dark hair and hazel eyes. Daisy had a careworn expression that came less with age than carrying too much responsibility too soon. Even before our deadbeat father left she'd been looking out for the rest of us. When Mom began her revolving door of low-paying jobs, Daisy had become the de facto matriarch. Then she married and had two sets of identical twin boys who deepened the lines we'd started. Nonetheless she was pretty, especially when she offered a rare smile as she did now.

Iris was striking, rather than pretty. Her hair was still naturally dark and fell in artful waves tonight over the straps of her little black dress. She'd always been well put together, but lately she'd upped her game, perhaps sensing that she needed to be a walking billboard for the salon. For many years she'd been a curator in the small, quirky museums that dotted hill country, but the work paid a pittance and she'd been pondering a career change for ages.

"I'm glad to hear all publicity is good publicity," I said. "Because I've had so much of it lately. That must mean I can expect an influx of new guests anytime."

Daisy sighed. She still felt bad over her dealings with Lloyd Boyce, the local dogcatcher and first murder victim on my land. "Let's introduce you around so you can spread the word about the inn," she said. "You were away so long that you need to meet the movers and shakers."

"There are movers and shakers in Clover Grove? Why am I just hearing this now?" I let her tow me away from Mom and Iris. "Or do you just mean the so-called pillars of the community, like the bridge club?"

The Bridge Buddies had recently stayed for a weekend

at the inn, during which the third murder occurred. The tension made the club's long-simmering feud erupt and they'd disbanded, at least temporarily.

"The real influencers aren't always who you'd expect," Daisy said. "They keep a low profile and do nice things for people without looking for glory."

There was a row of folding chairs across the back of the salon. My sisters and Jilly had hung filmy curtain panels in front of the washing stations to make the small shop more party-friendly. People were rapidly filling the open space around the two prominent styling chairs. In fact, it was so crowded that Violet propped open the door to allow people to spill out onto the sidewalk. Keats threw back his head to sniff the breeze and then gave a little whine.

"I know, buddy," I said. "I'm claustrophobic, too. Hang in there."

Daisy pinched my arm. "Publicity, remember? You want to keep the farm afloat and here's someone who knows almost everyone in hill country. She's one of our most distinguished residents."

The woman sitting on the folding chair looked surprisingly tranquil, given the crowd and the setting. "Daisy," she said, in a deep, rich voice. "How nice to see you, dear. You were so kind to me after my surgery last winter. I haven't thanked you enough."

"You thanked me plenty, Miss Bingham," my sister said. "I don't believe you've met my baby sister, Ivy. And this is her dog, Keats."

"Of course I've met Ivy," Miss Bingham said. "But she was just a pretty young girl then. Always so quiet and well-behaved. It's nice to see you again, dear."

"I remember you, too, Miss Bingham," I said. "You came

to our fundraisers for the local animal rescue. Once you gave us a hundred dollars, and I'd never felt so lucky."

She beamed at me. "I've never been able to resist a pet charity. And while cats are my true weakness, I had plenty of dogs in my time." She braced herself on a four-pronged cane and waved to summon a balding middle-aged man and a woman with nicely highlighted blonde hair and a care-worn look like Daisy's. "This is my nephew, Michael, and his wife, Caroline," Miss Bingham said. "I'm always so happy when they visit Clover Grove."

"It's good to be back," Michael said with a pleasant smile. "I miss the old manor though, Aunt Hazel."

"Times change," she said, sighing and looking down. "Are you as brilliant as everyone says, Keats? I've heard stories."

His tail swished briskly, giving Miss Bingham an enthusiastic pass in the character department. When it brushed Michael's pant leg, his wife eased him away into the crowd. Not a dog lover, clearly, but more tactful than most.

"Keats is brilliant," I told Miss Bingham. "Rescuing him was another lucky moment for me."

The old woman gave me a keen glance. "Except for your injuries. You paid a high price, didn't you?"

Keats tipped up his muzzle and his brown eye filled me with sunlight from the soles of my dirty feet to the crown of my head. "No regrets, Miss Bingham. He's the best dog in the world."

The best dog in the world darted away suddenly. There was a black-and-white flash between the sea of legs and then I caught a glimpse of orange.

Not just any orange: fluffy marmalade with a magnificent tail.

"Oh no! It's Percy!"

"Percy?" Daisy said. "You mean the cat you just adopted from Edna's feral colony?"

I knelt, trying to track the pair. "He adopted me. But yes."

Seeing Keats somewhat successfully herding the cat toward me, I looked up to find Miss Bingham watching me with eyes as sharp as a crow's. "You brought a cat to a party, Ivy?"

I heard Mom's scream and shut my eyes briefly. "I'm not that far gone, Miss Bingham. Percy must have stowed away in the car as I dealt with an issue on the farm."

An issue Percy had caused by releasing the llama. I couldn't help but wonder if he'd created that diversion for the very purpose of slipping into the car. He hated being left behind. Now I realized Keats had tried to tell me something was up during the drive and I didn't listen. Then, when I was dusting off my dress after parking, the cat must have slipped out. For an eye-catching feline, he could move like a shadow.

At the moment Percy had no compunction about making a spectacle of himself. To avoid Keats, he leapt onto an old man's lap and then launched himself onto a high shelf that held a display of hair products. From there, the cat picked his way nonchalantly toward me, tail high, and completely full of himself.

When he was behind Miss Bingham, he sat and wrapped his tail around his paws, giving me what could only be called a Cheshire grin.

"Oh, Percy. Really?" I shook my head in disgust as Keats pressed into my legs mumbling canine profanity.

"That," Miss Bingham said, "is a marvelous cat. And obviously as clever as your dog."

Keats gave a sharp squeak of protest.

"*Nearly* as clever," she corrected seamlessly. "Ivy, you obviously have a special connection with animals. I admire that in a person. Hannah Pemberton and I hit it off for the same reason."

I tore my eyes away from Percy reluctantly. He was scanning the room with eyes as eerily green as Keats' blue one. There was no telling what he would do. I was quite sure what Mom would do, however, and she was snaking toward me now. Hands kept reaching out to stop her. Some of those hands wanted to congratulate her, while the many hands of my siblings tried to deter her.

"I'd love to hear about your friendship with Hannah," I said. "But first I'm going to have to figure out how to get the cat back into the car."

Miss Bingham gave an infectious laugh. "Good luck, dear. I suspect that cat is going to do what he wants, when he wants."

Percy unfurled his fluffy tail, stood up, and then arched his back. He opened his mouth and out came an odd pop of sound. It was a combination of a hiss and a spit, and it was enough to bring Keats' hackles up, too.

I turned to see what the fuss was about and found a woman standing right behind me. Her eyes narrowed to feline slits and her gray corkscrew curls seemed to puff like hackles, too.

"People like you don't deserve pets," she said. "I'm going to report you to Animal Services."

CHAPTER THREE

I straightened my shoulders, grateful to Jilly's heels for giving me even more of a height advantage.

"Pardon me?" I said.

"You heard me." Medusa doubled down on the fierce glare. "What were you thinking bringing a cat into town to run around? He could be hit by a car, or poisoned by shampoo."

"First of all, I didn't bring him. He brought himself." I immediately regretted how crazy that sounded. "He stowed away in the car while I was rounding up a runaway llama."

The woman smiled, vindicated by the new information. "A runaway llama? So you have zero control over any of your animals?"

My mouth opened but Daisy squeezed my forearm to hold back the hot words gathering like lava in my throat. Since my concussion, I'd had a bit of trouble with impulse control and Jilly and Daisy tag-teamed to keep me from stepping on local landmines. I couldn't afford to offend the many people who offended me if I wanted my business to grow and my reputation to shine.

Miss Bingham raised a hand that was gnarled with age but glittering with pretty rings. "Portia. Dear, please. I've known Ivy Galloway since she was a child and she's always been an animal lover, just like you."

"Just like me?" Portia's words popped out with the indignant tone of Percy's commentary earlier. "I am a trained and certified cat care provider. If I treated animals like this, I'd have no business at all."

"Oh, *you're* The Cat Lady," I said. "I've heard about you."

Daisy jumped in. "Portia Parson has run a pet-sitting service in Clover Grove for years."

"A *cat*-sitting service," Portia corrected. "And for decades."

Miss Bingham's bejewelled hand clutched Portia's arm in the same way Daisy still held mine. They were both trying to contain a firefight.

"Portia's been a godsend to me," the old woman said. "I used to travel often and I always knew my pets were pampered. All cats adore her."

"Isn't that wonderful, Ivy?" Daisy said. "It sounds like you and Portia have a lot in common."

Before I could speak, Portia jumped in. "We have *nothing* in common. Ivy's animals are in constant peril from miscreants and murderers." She stared up at Percy who stared back, still puffed. Perhaps she'd met the one cat who didn't adore her. "I've been after the County to intervene. I'm starting a petition."

"A petition! How dare you!"

Two voices overlapped with mine. Throw in Keats' shrill yip, and it was loud enough to silence a crowded room.

One of the speakers continued before I could. "Portia

Parson, you have some nerve coming into my establishment and insulting my daughter." Mom's glare threw off enough sparks to rival Portia's. "Ivy's risked her life for these animals again and again."

"That's exactly my point. There shouldn't be any risk to animals at Runaway Farm," Portia persisted. "Yet it's all front-page news over there. I'm no fan of dogs, but this one shouldn't need to throw himself in harm's way to protect you, Ivy Galloway. You don't deserve a dog like him."

Suddenly I felt small. Minuscule. Ashamed. Keats rubbed against my leg and moaned.

"Portia Parson, you have crossed the line," Mom said. "Take your fright wig and go. Don't ever cross Bloomers' doorstep again, or so help me, I'll—"

"Mom!" This time Daisy's voice and mine overlapped. I pulled my arm from my sister's grasp and continued. "Don't let The Cat Lady ruin your big night on my account. She's only saying what lots of people in Clover Grove think."

"Darn right," Portia muttered.

"Portia, enough," Miss Bingham said. "You've said your piece and while I think the world of you, I believe you're wrong about Ivy."

Portia tossed her wild hair and shrugged. "We'll let the petition decide. If I get enough signatures, the County will need to evacuate your farm."

Asher—tall, fair, blue-eyed and the literal golden boy of the family—responded to Jilly's frenzied beckoning in time to hear Portia's threat.

Since I couldn't form the words, Jilly did it for me. "Can the County do that, Asher?"

My brother's nearly perpetual smile flashed off and he straightened in his uniform. He'd had to snatch an hour while on duty, and Kellan had texted to say he couldn't come at all.

"They'd have a heck of a time getting support for a move like that with so many vocal homesteaders who keep livestock," Asher said. "There's enough going on around here without pestering a hobby farmer whose inn contributes to the economy."

"Too bad about the online smear campaign someone's starting about the inn," Portia said, with a smug smile. "Not me, of course. The only thing Ivy's contributed to Clover Grove is gossip."

Now my brother moved forward, pressing Portia back with his height and presence. Although his colleagues called him the golden retriever of cops, he still knew how to throw his weight around when his family was under attack.

"Miss Parson, if you don't like the company, perhaps it's time to move along," he said.

"I'm not leaving until that cat is safe," she said, glancing up.

Percy was nowhere to be seen now. Having had his second big show of the evening, he'd retreated to plan his next event.

"I'll make sure the cat gets home safely," Asher said. "You have my assurance. Would you like a ride home? I'd be happy to take you, but I do have the squad car."

Portia's frizz seemed to collapse. "No thank you, officer. If I'm not welcome here, I'll make my own way."

"Of course you're welcome here," Iris said, stepping out from behind Asher. "Don't be silly, Portia. In fact, I'd love to have you back for a complimentary haircut and spa treatment."

"I don't need a haircut," Portia said.

"Everyone needs a haircut," Iris said. "It freshens your

outlook like nothing else. Plus I have a miracle conditioner that'll make your hair glitter like a Christmas angel's. Just give me a try."

Jilly swept her golden hair over one shoulder to show it off for Portia. "I'm living proof of that. I don't know how Iris does it."

Mom straightened her shoulders. "I take—"

"Great pleasure in showing you how hospitable Bloomers can be," Iris interrupted smoothly.

My eyes widened as Iris guided Portia to the front desk and wrote something on a business card.

"Iris will do well for herself," Miss Bingham said. "I'll send all my friends here. They drifted away because of the previous owner's difficult clientele."

Mom's hackles dropped instantly. "Thank you, Miss Bingham. Word of mouth like that is pure gold."

There was a sudden streak of orange as Percy leapt and landed lightly on the old woman's lap. Her gasp turned into a chuckle as he turned several times and settled. "Oh, he's purring," she said, as her gleaming rings ran over his sleek side. "What a delightful ginger gentleman." Looking up at me, she added, "Ivy, I can see your animals are gloriously happy and well cared for. Don't you worry about Portia one bit. I can handle her."

"Are you sure?" I asked. "Because word of mouth like a petition is pure coal."

"Out of coal comes diamonds," Miss Bingham said, lifting a hand from Percy to flash a few sparkling carats. "You're being tested and you will prevail."

Keats moved in so that Miss Bingham could run some jewels over his head.

"Keats, leave it," I said, worried the furry enemies would pull a stunt on the stage of Miss Bingham's lap.

"Never mind," the old lady said. "That's why God gave me two hands."

Michael Bingham tapped her shoulder. "Are you ready to leave, Aunt Hazel?"

"Yes, but you and Caroline stay and have fun," she said. "Parties are few and far between in Clover Grove." Then she looked up at my brother. "I'll take that ride, young man. Turn on the siren and let's give everyone at the seniors' home a thrill when we arrive."

CHAPTER FOUR

The next afternoon was gorgeous when Kellan Harper and I set off for a walk. Fall weather like this was a trick that hill country visitors might fall for: balmy and brilliantly colorful, with the barest hint of a breeze that carried the scent of moss and anything else that hadn't put up closed signs for the season. As someone born and bred in Clover Grove, I knew this was just the last kiss before the punch of winter. Hometown kids learned to wring the most from the days before the parkas came out.

Kellan knew this well, too, which was probably why his expression flipped from cheerful to pensive and back. Winters were no joke in these parts and made police work even harder.

There was no staying pensive for long when Keats was on the case, however. The dog was racing from bush to boulder to thicket, crouching and darting, and then repeating the maneuver. I shook my head as he blatantly stalked Kellan, rounding him up as if he were a fleecy sheep instead of the chief of police.

I'd expected the dog's mission to drive our little herd of

two together to end when Kellan and I started dating regularly. Instead, it escalated, as if to say, "Get on with this, already." I suppose when sheepdogs brought livestock together nature took its course quickly. Humans with a history like ours took a little longer to get over old wounds.

Unlike Keats, I was quite happy with the pace of the relationship. Kellan and I had been high school sweethearts, hit the rocks as college freshmen, and only recently started seeing each other after more than a decade. Further, we'd clashed often in the months since I'd been home because he thought I was interfering in his investigations of the three murders that had taken place on or around the farm.

He wasn't wrong. Although I disagreed with his assertion that I was utterly reckless, I'd definitely stuck my nose in where it didn't legally belong. Who could blame me when my farm, livestock and reputation were on the line? Besides, what Kellan didn't like to acknowledge was that when Keats stuck *his* long nose into these investigations, the dog not only turned up clues the police hadn't, he also helped to take down the perpetrator in each case.

Even so, I wouldn't have blamed Kellan for wanting to leave our old romance buried as deep as the murder victims. Instead, here he was, helping me check on a feral cat colony. All it had taken was one text and he was at the farm in under an hour. In uniform, no less.

"I'm glad you asked for backup instead of running off half-cocked to investigate on your own," he said, apparently oblivious to his black-and-white stalker. "It's good to see some caution emerging."

The smirk on his face might have been annoying if he weren't so darned handsome. Chief Harper—better known by Jilly as "Chief Hottie"—was a far cry from Kellan the high school boy-next-door. There were moments where I felt like I was batting out of my league, but I wouldn't let that stop me. Keats seemed to think Chief Hottie was getting a decent deal and the dog had great instincts. If he thought Kellan and I should herd up, who was I to argue?

"I'm not scared of going over to feed Edna's cats," I said. "Jilly offered to come and of course Keats has me covered."

"No?" He looked a little disappointed. Maybe he wanted to be my hero instead of Keats.

"I wouldn't ask the chief of police to join me to feed a feral cat colony. He has more important matters to deal with." I grinned as Keats crept up, stiff-legged and belly low. "I was asking Kellan Harper, regular citizen."

His serious dark blue eyes lit up and he grinned, too. "You mean you were asking your boyfriend."

My face promptly burst into flames, or so it felt. My comment had been far clumsier than Keats' elegant attack.

"Something like that," I muttered, glad of an excuse to watch the dog versus meeting Kellan's eyes. "I wouldn't presume."

We'd only had a few dates and a few truly great kisses. I thought it would take far more than that to gain girlfriend status given all the barriers in our path. Kellan didn't share my natural affection for animals, for starters, and he certainly didn't care for farms. He was fastidious about his appearance and orderly in his behavior. Meanwhile, I was most comfortable in overalls and my life at Runaway Farm was about as far from orderly as it got. The way rescue animals kept appearing, it would only get worse.

"You can presume," Kellan said, coming closer without realizing that the move wasn't of his own free will. At least not entirely. "I'm sorry I got to the party too late to back you last night. There was a break-in at the hunting supply store, and a couple of rifles are missing."

"No worries," I said, glad of the distraction. "I hope no one gets hurt."

Finally, Keats made his final lunge from behind. In the same moment, there was a flash of orange on the path before us. The canine missile shot between us and collided at our feet with a puff of marmalade fur and a cacophonous blend of growling, snarling, hissing and spitting. Kellan raised his arms, either to steady me or find his own balance, and I did the same. One more thrash of fur sent us reeling into each other's arms.

My forehead hit Kellan's nose with a crunch that sounded painful. His muffled yelp confirmed it.

"Sorry, sorry," I blurted.

I tried to pull away but he didn't let me. Instead he put his hands on my shoulders and gave me a dazed look. "What just happened?"

"Sneak attack," I said. "Front and rear."

Percy released himself from the clinch and took off with Keats in pursuit.

"They're working in tandem now?" Kellan touched his nose and winced. "I don't stand a chance."

"Of course you do." I hoped he didn't mean "stand a chance" with me. "You're the youngest chief of police in the County and beyond. What border collie can make that claim?"

"I might be slightly smarter than the dog, but combined with the cat, I'm not sure."

Leaving his arm around my shoulder, he turned me forward and we started walking again.

"I don't think Percy's on the same scale," I said. "Although he has a mysterious agenda, like all cats."

There was high-pitched barking ahead as Keats vented his frustration. I knew from experience that Percy had jumped out of reach to taunt the dog from high places. Keats hadn't yet learned that his best strategy was to walk away and Percy would follow. The cat had flustered my brilliant dog in a way cold-blooded killers could not.

Kellan touched his nose and sighed again. "I suppose this is a 'love me, love my cat' situation?"

My face flushed again at the word "love." It was just an expression. There was no way he felt that way... yet. Someday I hoped he would. For now, I'd keep things light.

"And my alpaca," I said. "Plus my llamas, donkeys, cows, sheep, chickens, horse and goats."

"Thank you," he said, grinning.

"For what?"

"For leaving out the pig. There is no way I am warming to that sow. She'd take me down without even noticing."

"Don't be silly," I said. "She'd definitely notice. And she'd like it."

"Lovely." His arm tightened around my shoulders. "What's our mission today, anyway? Your text was deliberately vague."

"I was afraid you wouldn't come out for a missing cats report."

"Missing cats? How can you tell when there's over forty of them?"

"That's the thing: there's probably only twenty now. The tamest ones seem to have vanished since Edna left."

"They probably went back to the swamp. That's their home, right?"

I shook my head. "Edna's their home. Her food station is their home. The insulated shelters she installed are their home. They wouldn't just leave each other. Colony means they stay together."

We turned from the main path into a smaller one that

led to Edna's. The interconnected series of trails that ran between all the houses in the area were rough and best navigated by ATVs. At least I assumed so, since my rides in a golf cart were jarring enough to cause whiplash.

Kellan's head swivelled constantly now, aware that he might be ambushed at any second. "Well, what's *your* theory, Sherlock? Mine is that your Dorset Hills rescue brigade has been pilfering felines."

"There's a plan in place to rehome most of the cats, and Edna agreed to it. But she wanted to be home to interview prospective owners. That's reasonable."

"But the pet brigade doesn't seem reasonable. After all, they call themselves the Rescue Mafia."

"They didn't choose that name themselves," I said. "And they'd tell me if they were deploying early."

"You're sure about that?"

His arm dropped as we circled Edna's house and an instant chill seeped into my bones. Kellan's job was all about law and order. The very existence of a Rescue Mafia was an insult to who he was.

"I'm sure. Something else is happening and I hoped you'd use your investigative skills to help me figure it out before any more cats go missing." I stopped walking as a terrible thought struck me. "What if someone's poisoning them?"

"More likely a predator," Kellan said. "There'd be evidence of poison, including remains."

"Wouldn't that be true of a predator, too?" Shivering, I crossed my arms. "It was a mistake to bring Keats over here."

"What about Percy? Doesn't he count?" Kellan smirked again before bending over to brush orange fur from his uniformed pant legs. No matter what he was wearing he ended up covered in more fur than I did. It was like the pets knew how much he hated it and did a full day's shedding all at once.

"Percy brought himself over. He was shut in the house when I left."

I called for the dog and cat and they both joined us at the feeding station Edna had built with her own hands before she left. For an octogenarian and former nurse, she had impressive carpentry skills. It was like a garage without walls, surrounded by fencing with small cat doors. Half a dozen insulated boxes offered all-season accommodation should it be needed.

"Hey," I said, as we unlatched the gate and walked into the enclosure. "Something's changed."

Pulling out my phone, I examined the photo I'd taken the day before to record the exact positioning of bowls. I'd suspected things had been moving around in ways cats couldn't really manage. The change was too precise for predators. It was as if someone just preferred a different setup. The kibble looked different, too.

The dog and cat initially followed us inside and then turned back. Keats' ruff came up first but Percy's wasn't far behind. Suddenly they both bolted into the bush, where we heard sticks breaking and then an odd clattering sound.

"If that's a fox, it's a big one," I said. "Or a bear."

"Human," Kellan said. "Stay here while I go check things out."

I looked down at the metal bowl in my hand and said. "No need. I know exactly what's happening."

He looked over my shoulder as I pinched finger and thumb together to pull two long strands of hair out of the bowl: wiry gray corkscrews.

"Portia Parson," I said. "The Cat Lady. And unless I'm much mistaken, that rattling sound was a plastic cat carrier."

"Oh great," Kellan said. "Now Clover Grove has its own rescue mafia. My job just got even more complicated."

"At least she didn't steal rifles," I said. "At least I hope not."

"Me too," he said. "Because I'm going to pay her a little visit."

CHAPTER FIVE

"**O**uch! Can you—" Jilly's voice cut off abruptly as we hit another rock. After a second or two she added, "Slow down."

"Sure, sure," I said. "There's no hurry."

"Right. And I can't help thinking it would be better to take it easy in this particular vehicle," Jilly said. I could feel her staring at the side of my head but it was too dark to see, even if I dared take my eyes off the small circle of light cast by the golf cart's headlights. "If you don't care about your own safety, maybe think about mine. Not to mention theirs."

Her fingers released their tight grip on the dashboard just long enough to jerk her thumb at the back seat. Keats and Percy had begun our journey on the cushions but gravitated quickly to the footwells.

"I don't hear them complaining," I said, grinning as I slowed down. "Where's your sense of adventure?"

"Excuse me?" Her voice was a bit shrill. "I've joined you on many a crazy adventure, Ivy Galloway. But I have to say I prefer jolting around in the pickup to this. At least the truck won't tip over."

"I'll crawl, don't worry. Just got carried away for a second."

"For a second..." she grumbled under her breath in a way that reminded me of Keats. "Try six months."

"Well, who does she think she is, capturing Edna's cats and making decisions about their welfare? It's none of her business. She's a stuck-up—"

A particularly large rock choked off my next word.

"I agree, which is the only reason I joined you," Jilly said. "But we could have parked out at the highway and walked in from there."

"Both of my vehicles are recognizable, particularly by Portia Parson. She'd be on the lookout." I steered the golf cart carefully around a hairpin turn and headed south on the trail. "Luckily this network covers half of Clover Grove. It supposedly dates back to rum-running prohibition days. Kellan says it's still used by those who want to have some adult beverages and avoid the law."

"Fabulous," Jilly said. "So we might encounter a drunk teenage driver at any time."

"Think positively," I said. "It's far more likely a big root would kill us first. Anyway, I mapped out the route to Portia's carefully and we're almost there. Remember the plan. We park in the bush and I sneak over to the house with Keats and Percy to do a quick reconnaissance. Then we're gone."

"Kellan said he'd drop by and see Portia. Wasn't that enough?"

"Do you really think Kellan would recognize any of Edna's cats? His eyes glazed over as I flicked through the photos. It was like a stupor."

"He's not a pet lover," she said. "Besides, it takes a week or two to get to know them by sight. Then they're as unique as snowflakes, I admit. Except for the gray tabbies. There are so many of them I still get stumped."

"Me too. I'm glad Percy is so distinctive. He's a very handsome cat."

"Sshhh," Jilly said. "You'll hurt Keats' feelings. His nose is already out of joint."

"Well, Keats is even more distinctive." I raised my voice so the dog could hear me over the whirring motor and thudding sound of the wheels on the path. "That blue eye is downright magical."

"Much better," Jilly said. "Don't forget your HR skills. Gotta keep the team happy so we operate like a well-oiled machine."

"I never expected my squad to include a genius border collie, let alone an audacious cat." After navigating a particularly treacherous hill, I added, "But it sure beats the Flordale team. I trust you and these boys with my life."

"Exactly. So be sure to offer lots of validation and rewards." She gave a little scream as we tilted perilously. "Otherwise they'll be asking me to headhunt new jobs. And you know who'd snap Keats up in a heartbeat? Cori Hogan."

"Don't even go there, Jilly Blackwood. No one comes between me and Keats. Ever."

"Except Kellan, maybe?" I was surprised at how cunning she could be in life-and-death circumstances.

"Kellan won't come between Keats and me. He can stand on my other side. With you."

I rather liked that mental image. It reminded me of a wedding party. Shaking my head, I tried to dispel the notion. Romance was the last thing I should be thinking of in the middle of an important mission.

"Sounds good," Jilly said. "Now focus."

"Yeah. We're almost there." I slowed even more as we rounded the last bend and then tucked the cart into the bushes. Turning off the lights, I whispered, "It's the old Bingham manor."

Jilly strained to peek through the branches but it was too dark. "How'd she luck out on this place? It doesn't seem like cat sitting would finance a manor?"

"Same way I lucked out on Runaway Farm. Miss Bingham took a shine to Portia and offered her a deal on the place in exchange for caring for her six cats. After breaking her hip last year, Miss Bingham decided to move into Sunny Acres retirement villa. This way she still gets to visit."

"I hope someone offers me a manor some day," Jilly said. "More like a sweet little bistro that needs to be rescued."

"It could happen and you deserve it," I said, patting her arm. "In the meantime, you keep honing your chops in my lucky kitchen with all its granite and marble. You'll never see the likes of that pantry again."

"True," she said. "Now, hurry up and slow down, okay?"

I laughed quietly as I got out of the cart. "I like the way you think, my friend."

Keats and Percy didn't wait to be invited. I heard the rustle of dry leaves and felt fur on either side as they brushed past. It figured they'd want to be ahead of me. I had no issue with Keats taking a few liberties, but Percy could be a liability here. A cat like him would be like... well, catnip to the Cat Lady.

"Stay with me," I hissed into the darkness, and both animals circled back to brush my legs again. "Thank you.

I've got enough to worry about without losing track of you. Just in and out, okay? I promised Jilly."

I'd also more or less promised Kellan not to interfere. The "more or less" part was crucial. My exact wording had deliberately left wiggle room. After a decade in HR, I knew the value of a loophole.

The old manor looked ominous in the darkness, but I remembered seeing the place during its glory days. It had been everything a country manor should be, with golden brown brick, white trim and coppery accents. A quick flick of my phone light told me it needed more care than Portia Parson could afford. Like me, she was batting out of her league with real estate. Cat-sitting was probably about as lucrative as my innkeeping had been so far. My nest egg from selling my condo in Boston was all but gone and if business didn't pick up soon, I'd be forced to get a regular job in town to stay afloat.

With one pet on either side, I crept to the side of the manor, where the ground floor windows were smaller. If Portia were home, she'd likely be in the living room at the front of the house, chilling with a reality TV show.

"Easy," I whispered, stooping as I moved closer. Every crunch of leaves underfoot sounded like cannon fire. Autumn wasn't the best season for snooping, but at least there were no mosquitos.

Under the window, I dropped to my knees and waited till I caught my breath. Then I gripped the windowsill, feeling the chipped paint under cold fingertips, and slowly pulled myself up to peer into the house. Pressing my forehead nearly to the glass, I waited for my eyes to adjust.

The room inside was well lit. There was a grand oak dining table that had to be 12 feet long in the center of the room. What I saw sitting on that fine antique made me release the windowsill and drop hard onto my butt on the damp earth. I almost let out a scream but Keats gave me a sharp poke with his long muzzle and mumbled something I took to mean, "Shut it."

Percy, on the other hand, leapt up to the windowsill and released a long low hiss. Then he jumped down, ran a few yards and looked back.

The order to evacuate was loud and clear, and I was willing to let the cat call the shots.

CHAPTER SIX

Jilly took a breath that sounded like a solid nine-count and let it out slowly as we walked down Clover Grove's main street toward Bloomers. Every week there seemed to be more quaint, antique-style storefronts that resembled those of Dorset Hills, or Dog Town, the neighboring city that attracted more tourism dollars than we ever could. I understood the County's desire to capitalize on Dog Town's popularity, but I wished they'd find a unique claim to fame. Clover Grove had plenty of virtues that Dorset Hills could no longer claim because it was too big and commercialized now. Our sweet niche was there, waiting to be exploited, and it started with the home-steading craze, if you asked me.

"Do you want me to do the talking?" Jilly asked, when I was silent for too long. She didn't want me ruminating because rumination led to blurting. And blurting led to bad press for the inn.

"I'd like to give it a try," I said. "Although I'm still spit-ting mad."

"And rightly so, but you know as well as I do that it's

always better to negotiate peacefully. I really think you can talk your way through this if you keep a cool head."

I looked down at Keats. "Can we do that, buddy? How cool do you feel today?"

His ears were forward and tail up. A good sign.

"All right then," Jilly said. "I'll put my energy into handling your mother."

"That's more than half the battle, my friend. Thank you."

A chime sounded as I pushed open the salon door and walked inside, sandwiched by Keats in front and Jilly behind. Percy wasn't invited and he'd taken the rejection hard. He was trapped and wailing in the laundry room when we left, and I half expected him to find a way out. Sometimes it seemed like he knew how to teleport or at least fold himself into a paper airplane and fly away. But I knew he was just observant and opportunistic. He could tell when my attention was focussed elsewhere. With all the distractions in my life, and my brain still not operating at full warp, it probably wasn't that hard for a smart cat to escape.

Percy's bigger challenge was evading the dog's detection. As farfetched as it sounded, I believed Percy had deliberately created his chance to joyride into town for the salon launch by decoying the dog with the runaway llama. If so, that would make this feline Houdini a bigger challenge than my sly sow, Wilma, though decidedly less lethal.

It was disheartening that my animals could often outthink me, but at least I generally handled people with skill. My years spent in the trenches of HR had taught me more than I ever wanted to know about the workings of the human mind.

"Ivy, darling!" Mom came around the counter with a

rapid click-click of stilettos. She'd covered a red skirt and plunging sweater with a white lab coat—the uniform of the late-blooming lady barber, I presumed. "What a surprise!"

The only surprise was her overacting. Mom was as sly and slippery as Wilma and Percy. Either she was creating drama to spice things up, or she was actually nervous. Maybe Jilly was right about Mom being so committed to the salon venture that her normal nonchalance had vanished. She no longer had the luxury of fanning the flames of gossip just for fun. Word of mouth and a good reputation meant everything in a small town, so she'd have to do a complete U-turn if she wanted to drive business. Given her notorious challenges behind the wheel of Buttercup, this would be interesting.

For once, I empathized with Mom. It wasn't easy to court public favor in Clover Grove when you had a history. Putting your fate into the hands—or more specifically, the mouths—of the local citizenry was frustrating. Today, we'd need to dig deep and possibly even grovel, because Iris's special guest could do our reputations a world of harm. Fortunately, we could fall back on Jilly, who rarely made a social misstep. She could soothe the worst egos and leave people thinking her big ideas emerged from their own small minds, like genies from a crusty old beer bottle.

I trusted her implicitly, but my stomach still sank when I saw the wild gray mop in the red vinyl styling chair. Iris had brushed Portia Parson's hair into a frizzy cloud that hung nearly to her waist.

"Hey, Mom. How's it going?" I summoned my blandest smile and hauled out my old HR skills. I could fake it with the best in my day. To channel my inner professional, I'd even worn my old suit jacket. It hung open and unbuttoned, yet I felt like I was suffocating. "Oh, hi there, Portia. Sorry for interrupting your makeover. Jilly just wanted to drop off some cookies for Mom."

Jilly pried the cover off the batch of still-warm cookies and waved the container to send a waft of sweet chocolatey air toward the styling chair. Portia frowned and fanned one hand, as if dispersing the stench of cat litter.

"I don't eat cookies." She scanned Jilly and me. "Carbs are the devil's work."

I stuck my face in my elbow and pretended to sneeze to disguise my snort of laughter. Jilly and I had both lost weight because we were often too busy to do more than sample the fine cuisine at the inn. On top of that, hard labor had given me "pipes." As a formerly pasty exec, I took pride in flexing sometimes. I'd earned it.

"I'd love one," Iris said. "Put them on the counter for when I finish Portia's transformation."

"In Clover Grove we just call it a haircut," Portia said. "Affectations won't take you far, Iris."

"A good haircut truly has the power to transform," Jilly said, easing up beside Portia's chair. "My hair is nearly as curly as yours, Portia, but Iris has tamed it with her magic scissors and products."

The Cat Lady eyed Iris's gold-handled scissors and grunted. "I don't have time to worry about my hair. I'm only here because she offered me a free cut. Free is the only magic I need."

"I hear you," I said. "I'm always looking for ways to squeeze a penny now that I have so many mouths to feed." I gestured to Keats, whose tail swished, as it always did in Mom's presence. "I assume you have a few pets, too, Portia?"

She gave me a sharp-eyed stare that told me I'd have to "subtle down." Portia was annoying but she wasn't stupid.

"I took over Miss Bingham's cats when she sold me the manor," she said. "It was part of the deal."

Nicely done. She got full points for telling the truth while covering a huge lie. I had another wily critter on my hands.

"What a lucky break that was," Mom trilled, grabbing a glass pitcher of water and lemon slices. "Miss Bingham was so generous with you." Portia started to speak but Mom blundered on. "Of course, you'd earned that break with years of dedicated service."

"Exactly right." Portia eyed Mom now, as if looking for the arrow in the lemon water. "And what seems like a great deal on the surface isn't the full story. It's one problem after another in an old place like that."

"Same with the farm," I said. "I got one heck of lucky break, but it's costly to keep the place up."

Portia's wary eyes moved from one of us to the other, so distracted that she failed to notice Iris snipping. One inch turned into three and then five. Gray frizz fell to the gleaming hardwood floor and formed tumbleweeds that Keats half-heartedly chased. He'd taken issue with Portia at the launch but he didn't seem put off by her now.

"Our situations are nothing alike, Ivy," Portia said at last. "You swanned in and took advantage of a heart-broken heiress after one dog rescue. I spent over twenty years couch surfing at one place after another serving the cats of Clover Grove. I *earned* that break. It wasn't luck at all."

"Well, it couldn't have happened to a more committed animal lover," Jilly said, her voice becoming velvety.

"*Cat* lover," Portia corrected, glancing at Keats with thinly veiled disgust. "Dogs torment cats and make my job harder. I saw how this one harassed the marmalade tabby you brought in here. He's one heck of a cat and he deserves better."

Jilly gripped my arm to push the words back up the pipe.

"Keats and Percy are still adjusting to each other," Jilly said. "Believe it or not, the cat has the upper paw. He's so clever and brave."

Portia gave a grudging nod. "I could see that. Where did you find him?"

Jilly squeezed my arm harder before answering for me. "He found us. One day he was just sitting on the porch swing and he never left."

"You probably stick him in the barn to deal with rats," Portia said.

This time my laugh slipped out before I could stop it. "He slept on the pillow beside mine last night. I woke up with orange fur in my eyelashes."

For a second her hard expression softened. "He'd be happier with other cats, though. They're pack animals."

I got my sleeve up in time to muffle the next snort, which allowed Jilly to pick up again.

"We're hoping the two barn cats Hannah left behind come home soon," she said. "Of course, they'll be welcome in the house, too. I've always been a cat lover."

"Me too," Mom said. She brushed her white lab coat with one hand, exposing her blatant lie. "They're fascinating creatures, aren't they?"

I gave her a look and she raised well-manicured eyebrows defiantly. Before we could take the stare-off any further, however, Wayne Flagg, her client with the dyed hair, stepped into the shop.

He turned to me after greeting my mother. "There is nothing more relaxing than an old-fashioned straightedge shave, and the only other barber in town stopped offering it two years ago. Your mother's a godsend and word's getting around fast."

Mom was suddenly all business, whisking Wayne into a striped cape and easing him back in the chair till he was nearly horizontal. She applied a woodsy-scented lotion and wrapped his face in a hot towel, murmuring in the way I sometimes talked to Keats. It was like she was in her own little world, which was perfect because she was out of mine for the moment.

Meeting Portia's eyes in the mirror, I finally got to the point. "I can see why my neighbor, Edna Evans, started looking after a feral cat colony this year. Although it was a huge amount of work for a woman her age, she grew to love each and every one. They all had names."

Portia turned so fast that Iris barely yanked the scissors back in time to avoid a styling fatality.

"I heard about that colony," she said. "No cat should live in a swamp, even in summer. What was Edna thinking gathering them up like that?"

"Well, like you said, they're pack animals." I suppressed a smirk. "They gathered themselves once the word got out about the free food. Edna also oversaw their veterinary care and took the ones she could trap to be neutered and vaccinated. It cost her a bomb and she was worried about winter coming. There's a plan in place for when she's back from Australia."

"And what plan is that?" Portia's tone was imperious. "There's no way Edna Evans would let so many cats inside. She practically dipped us in rubbing alcohol before vaccinating us when she was school nurse." Her full-body shudder was visible through her Bloomers gown. "She terrified me then."

"Edna's a different person now," I said. "Much of that comes from the cats. Loving animals can transform people even more than a haircut, right?"

Jilly squeezed my arm again, warning me not to overdo it. But Portia's furrowed brow smoothed, and she said, "I guess. For some people."

"That's why I'm trying my best to keep Edna's cats safe and happy till she gets back. She's going to find good homes for them but wants to interview the new owners herself."

I was close, so close... Portia's eyes glazed, as if she were recalibrating. She couldn't keep that many cats herself without eventually attracting the County's notice and having Animal Services seize them. Knowing that Edna intended to place them in loving homes, she might actually return them.

"It's not easy finding homes for feral cats, though," she said. "Everyone wants a cute kitten. They don't see the potential."

"Agreed. These cats can be so affectionate when they finally get the kindness they deserve. Edna has more connections than you might think. Huckleberry Marsh was about staying under the County's radar, which takes work."

Portia's eyes dropped. "Yeah."

"I had a run-in with Tess Blade, the Animal Services field officer, and she was one tough cookie," I said. "I wouldn't want her to get wind of the colony. What's the legal limit on cats in Clover Grove?"

"Six," Jilly supplied. "At least, indoor cats. I looked it up on the County website."

Now, Portia's eyes darted everywhere. Maybe she was picturing Tess Blade popping by the manor with her dogcatcher noose.

"That's why Edna needs to get these cats placed before

the County hears about them." I gave a huge sigh. "All it would take is one call, and the colony would be seized. It would break her heart."

Portia's eyes collided with mine again in the mirror. "I'd like to see Tess Blade try to seize any of my cats."

"I'm sure that would never happen," Jilly said. Her velvety tone became melodious, like a siren's. "Your cats live in luxury at the manor."

"It must be hard to keep it to six," I said. "Cats are so unique and addictive. They're like that old snack commercial: next handful's a whole new ball game."

"Bits and Bites," Jilly said. "Loved those."

Portia abruptly spun the chair with one foot till she faced me, making Iris step backward with the scissors.

"I'm a great marksman," she said. "If I found someone on my property without permission, I'd use them for target practice." She spun back just as abruptly. "Even you, Ivy Galloway." She slipped one hand out of the gown and made a circle with her index finger that included Jilly and Keats. "And your friends."

The threat was blatant enough to jar Mom out of her barbershop reverie. She turned away from Wayne with the straight edge in her hand. "Portia Parson, I already warned you about menacing my daughter. Let me extend that to include her friends."

"Portia didn't mean it that way," Jilly said, resting one hand on The Cat Lady's shoulder. "Emotions always run high when animal welfare's at stake."

Portia flicked Jilly's hand away and rose from the chair. "Or what, Dahlia? You'll slash me with that razor? That's not the free cut I had in mind."

She threw off the monogrammed cape with a flourish and looked down at the pile of hair on the floor. Iris had snipped about 10 inches off Portia's hair in layers. The other side was still untouched.

"Don't leave now," my sister pleaded. "I'll get that evened out in no time."

"This is perfect," Portia said, striding to the door. "I can show the town exactly what to expect from your salon." At the door, she fanned her face dramatically. "A crap job and a crapload of hassles. I can see the reviews, now: Here's one spa that'll leave you ugly and stressed."

"There's no fixing ugly," Mom muttered. Jilly locked her arm in a vice and Mom added, "An ugly mood, I mean."

"We can, though," Iris said, following Portia, and wringing her hands as best she could while still holding scissors. "I can fix an ugly mood in no time. Give me another chance, Portia."

"Bloomers is doomed," Portia called, as she walked out. "Better find a backup plan." She cast a last look of disgust over all of us. "And leave cat rescue to a professional, Ivy. Stick to what you're good at, which seems to be causing murder."

CHAPTER SEVEN

"Start over from the beginning," Cori Hogan said, as she paced back and forth at the base of the huge bronze statue of a chow chow. It was one of many such statues dotting—or blotting, depending on who you asked—the Dorset Hills landscape. The chow chow was all alone on the outskirts, which made it the ideal meeting spot for the Rescue Mafia.

I'd called in my first Rescue 911, and the tiny trainer had arrived promptly with Bridget Linsmore, Remi Malone, Evie Springdale and Andrea MacDuff. I'd met them all before, but it struck me anew that the word "mafia" didn't suit these women. They were attractive and down to earth. Cori was wearing jeans, a down jacket and her trademark black gloves with their orange middle fingers. Today those gloves gesticulated in a staccato manner that suggested she was either agitated or confused.

"Like I told you, last night I peeked into the old Bingham manor," I said. "I saw at least fifty cats, many of them from Edna's colony."

Cori plunked down at the base of the statue and leaned

against the massive dog's paw. I couldn't help thinking how cold that bronze must feel, even through her coat. "So you just happened to be driving your yellow jalopy by the old mansion and dropped in for a snoop?"

"Of course not," I said. "I wouldn't take Buttercup snooping. It would be like having my mom in the backseat."

"I'm her ride or die girl when it comes to trespassing," Jilly said. "We took the golf cart through the ATV trails."

"That must have been one heck of a ride," Cori said.

"It sure was," Jilly said. "My life flashed before my eyes more than once. And you don't see me sitting today, do you?"

Cori laughed, a rare enough sound in my short acquaintance with her. "I'll give you two some bonus points for courage," she said. "But then I'm docking you for stupidity. If you suspected something like that, you should have called us *before* your reckless jaunt, not after."

"What Cori means is that she prefers to do the reckless jaunting," Remi Malone said, picking up her sweet beagle Leo, and cradling him in her arms. I already recognized the move as a sign of nerves. "This discovery would have been another notch on her rescue belt."

Cori glared at her. "Put that dog down. If you can throw out shots like that, you're hardly overcome by anxiety."

"Habit," Remi said, grinning as she adjusted Leo for his maximum comfort.

"I don't need more notches in my rescue belt," Cori continued. "I can barely carry my laurels around as it is."

"Especially with your ego weighing you down," Evie Springdale said, adding her grin to Remi's. Her wild red curls were restrained in a knot but it looked like they were bristling to bust out. In fact, all the women exuded that kind of energy and I wondered if I did, too.

I shook my head at Remi and Evie. "You know you're both going to pay for insubordination, right?"

A grin found its way back to Cori's elfin face. "Ivy already knows me so well. Study and learn from her, dissenters."

Bridget moved toward me with Beau, her tall black dog. "Go on with the story, Ivy. I want to hear every last detail."

"Okay, let me back up a bit. Yesterday, I found a couple of long, gray corkscrew hairs in a cat food bowl at Edna's house. Then we heard a rattle in the bushes that sounded like a plastic cat carrier. I've heard that rattle a lot lately when taking Percy to his various engagements." I gestured at the fluffy orange cat, who was roaming around the circle of women, looking for cat lovers. He found one in Evie, who dropped to her knees, and then sat right down on the damp earth to welcome him into her lap. "I hadn't seen some of the friendlier cats in a few days and we wondered if Portia might be catnapping them."

"In this case, by 'we' she means Kellan Harper," Jilly said. "He offered to pay Portia a visit to investigate but Ivy took matters into her own golf cart."

"Can't blame her for wanting to check things out herself when she's the designated caregiver," Cori said, joining Bridget. They almost always ended up side by side, with Beau in between. "You can't trust a cop to do a rescuer's work. Especially a pet-hating cop."

"Kellan doesn't hate pets," I said. "He's..."

"Ambivalent?" Remi suggested. "A lot of our partners started out that way. You wear them down eventually."

I shrugged. "He knows it's a package deal. Love me, love my llamas."

"It's hard to love a llama," Evie said. "I got spit on more

times than I can count when we were filming Hannah's show."

"So, back to the story..." Bridget said. "You drove over to Portia's to see for yourself."

"Yeah. I honestly didn't expect her to have them on prominent display, but there were a dozen familiar faces in the dining room alone. Two of them were my own barn cats." I looked down at Keats and shook my head. "They preferred living in a swamp to Keats' company."

"Most cats can't handle a sheepdog's drive," Cori said.

"I felt bad about that, and I was going to try to convince them to give us another try. They won't fancy barn life after this, though. Portia's feeding the cats on the dining room table."

Every head shook in disapproval. Even these animal lovers had their limits, apparently.

"So, Portia Parson has stolen Edna's cats from the colony," Bridget said.

"Looks that way," I said. "I suppose it's possible they followed her home if she's the Pied Piper of cats, as people say. But I did hear that cat carrier, so I suspect she was picking off the tamest ones first and carrying them home. We heard an ATV after that, so she'd have made a lot of trips."

"Huh. How many of Edna's cats do you figure?" Cori asked.

"Maybe twenty? There were so many in the house and I didn't stay long enough to take photos. Percy wanted to get going."

Jilly picked up the story. "At the salon, we tried to give Portia an out. But she said Ivy—and even Edna—don't know how to care for these cats properly. She's convinced herself she's doing the right thing."

"Even after I explained there was a plan to rehome them," I said.

Cori turned quickly to stare at me with bright brown eyes. She reminded me of an eagle in a wren's clothing. I could be tough when I had to be, but it felt like a costume I put on, whereas Cori's fierceness went straight to the bone.

"We know Portia, of course," Bridget said. "She's always been quirky."

"*We're* quirky," Cori said. "Portia's strange."

"Well, pot, kettle and all that," Bridget said, smiling at her friend. "I used to turn to Portia for help placing cats, but the last couple of times I got a different vibe from her. Like she was distracted or stressed. Since stress and distraction make people unreliable, I decided to go elsewhere."

"Same," Cori said. "Shady vibe. I can't trust animals or my rep with shady."

"Well, if she's stressed and unreliable—and possibly shady—that's all the more reason to get the cats back," I said. "Edna's going to throw a hissy fit when she finds out what's happened."

Cori gave a dramatic slash with one orange flipping finger. "Edna forfeited her right to hiss when she pulled her recent stunt."

"I kind of admire her for that stunt," said Remi. Sweet-eyed Leo lolled in her arms, staring at Keats upside down. It was a lost cause, since Keats rarely wasted energy on other dogs. It was like he didn't even register their existence. Instead, his full focus was on Cori. Like most dogs, apparently, he'd fallen hard for the expert trainer. I wondered if he'd be tempted to ride off the farm and into the sunset with Cori if she invited him. Naturally, she drove a big truck with ease, and Keats did like a smooth ride. Still, if jolt came to stall, I was reasonably sure he'd choose me.

As if sensing my thoughts, Keats turned up his blue eye, stared at me briefly, and then turned to warm me with his brown eye. Sighing, I reached down and touched the soft fur between his ears. One day, I hoped to be truly worthy of this gifted dog. All I'd ever wanted was a simple pound-puppy, and instead I got the Maserati of the canine world. It set the bar high for a novice owner.

Cori started pacing again. "It sounds like The Cat Lady's gone rogue. She's well aware of our reputation for placing rescue animals, yet she's chosen to pack too many cats into her old house. That's not in the cats' best interests."

"Or hers," Bridget said. "Hiding them from Animal Services won't be easy. No wonder she seems stressed."

"If you've met Tess Blade, the new dogcatcher, you'd know why," I said.

Cori rubbed her forehead with one glove. "One day, Tess and I will go a few rounds with her catchpole. It won't be pretty, but I will prevail."

Jilly and I both laughed. I wouldn't want to challenge Tess to a duel, but I'd put good money on Cori for the win.

"So what can we do about Portia?" I asked. "Can we extract the cats?"

Cori stopped in front of me and set her gloves on her hips. "*You* can't do anything, Ivy. Not with Officer Boyfriend hanging around. Remember, I saw you at the bistro so stoned on cop pheromones you didn't notice your bra was covered in ketchup."

A snicker went around the clearing and Jilly's was loudest of all. Even Keats let his mouth drop open in a happy pant.

"Chief Hottie is what I call him," Jilly said. "But I'll attest that Kellan is a really good guy."

"I can handle myself," I said, trying to shove a cork into

my dignity as it drained rapidly. "I get in plenty of hot water with Chief Boyfriend, trust me."

Cori shook her head. "See, there's that word again. *Trust*. Our rescue work relies on trust and clear heads. We've had more than a decade of teamwork to build it."

"It's not personal," Bridget hastened to add. "We don't even trust our husbands most of the time. Not for rescue."

Remi came over and tried to offer me Leo, but noticed Keats' blue-eyed glare just in time. "I guess you have your own therapy dog," she said.

"Yeah, but I appreciate the offer." I scratched Keats' ears before turning back to Cori and Bridget. "All right, can *you* extract the cats?"

"Maybe," Cori said. "It's complicated. Portia is well connected, too. If these cats start appearing in shelters across the region, she's going to know it was us."

"We don't want to be on Portia's bad side," Bridget added. "She makes Cori look sweet."

"I am sweet... to animals and a few people of quality," Cori said. "But we have to do something. This isn't a good situation."

"Jilly and I want to help," I said. "Even from a distance. Maybe I can bait Portia out so you can do your thing."

"Maybe." Cori snapped her fingers silently to gather the team. "If we need you, we'll be in touch."

My poker face must have failed because Remi said, "Don't take it so hard. We're just trying to protect you."

"I don't want to be protected," I said.

"That's kind of the problem," Cori said, grinning. "You can be a loose cannon sometimes, Ivy. There's only room for one of those on a rescue team."

"Cori's already claimed that position," Evie said.

Bridget gave me a warm smile. "Trust, remember? You

know you can trust us. We've proven ourselves, haven't we?"

I nodded, looking down. Keats had started a stiff-legged stalk with Percy as his prey. Since the cat was lounging comfortably in Evie's lap, I snapped my fingers to get his attention. "Keats hates that cat," I said. "Sometimes I regret letting him inside."

"On the contrary," Cori said. "They're good buddies."

"Buddies?" I gave her a quizzical look. "They fight all the time."

"Like siblings, right? I don't have any, but I hear that's how it works." She tipped her head thoughtfully. "I watched as they followed you in here. They're communicating in ways you don't understand."

"And you do?" My tone was a little sharper than it needed to be, only because I was miffed over being a Mafia reject.

"I won't claim to speak cat fluently," Cori said. "But I know that Keats not only respects that cat, he also likes him. I'd go so far as to say they have a common purpose."

Keats ignored my warning and made a faux rush at Percy. I expected a scream from Evie but she stood at exactly the right moment for the cat to drop to the soil. Percy shot off like a rocket with the dog in pursuit.

"And that common purpose is chaos?" I asked.

Cori beckoned her friends and then shook her head. "I'm not going to spoon-feed you, Ivy. Hannah picked you to run her farm because you're supposed to be some kind of genius, with a genius dog. Now you also have a genius cat. Put your ego aside and figure it out."

"Ego! You have some—"

She held up a glove. "I have no ego when it comes to animals. I let them teach me, and mostly you do, too."

I let my hackles drop. "I guess."

"Observe. Open your mind." She led the posse down the trail. "Maybe you'll stay well ahead of the next murderer."

"Don't even say that," Jilly called after her. "You're jinxing us."

"Just saying what we all know," Cori said. "Ivy's calling isn't just the farm... it's solving crime. The trick is to stay more than one step ahead of the criminals."

"You got that right," I said, following her, with Keats and Percy kibitzing around my boots.

"Now we're speaking the same language," Cori said, offering a black wool thumbs-up over her shoulder.

CHAPTER EIGHT

"Ivy. It's Mom."

Normally my mother didn't bother identifying herself. She knew full well that my phone offered an ominous clash of cymbals whenever she called. It was the best ringtone ever, although it startled the more jittery livestock.

Luckily, she didn't call often. I had trained her well back in my HR grim reaper days, when I didn't have time for shenanigans. My thinking was that there were five other siblings to share the conversational load, since I carried most of the financial load of maintaining Mom's apartment and thrift store needs. Lately, she called more but was usually easily deterred by a casual mention of manure or animal behavior that she found offensive. On the other hand, she could now show up at the farm in person and her visits caused more damage than a simple phone call. I would have to revisit my strategy to take the new circumstances into account.

"I know it's you, Mom. The cymbals clashed. I heard thunder, too. There's a storm coming."

"This is no time for your little jokes, Ivy," she said. There was something different about her tone. Less cocky. "We need to talk."

I looked at the clock on the kitchen wall. Jilly and I had put in a long day after the Rescue Mafia meeting and were planning to crack open a bottle of wine with a late dinner. Jilly was sautéing chicken and vegetables to serve over pasta with some pesto she'd made in a huge batch to freeze. With more time on her hands, she had started putting up preserves like the homesteaders. By spring, she'd have a signature line available to tickle guests' taste buds and memories long after their stay at the inn.

"It is pretty late, Mom," I said. "Isn't it a date night?" I put the phone on speaker so that Jilly could share the pleasure of the jab and parry that characterized my chats with Mom. "Isn't *every* night a date night?"

"They do improv at The Tipsy Grape," Mom said. "Maybe the crowd there would appreciate your wit more than I do."

Normally Mom enjoyed sparring with me. She said I was the only one of her kids who gave her much of a challenge. "What's wrong?" I asked. "You sound a little edgy."

"You'd be edgy too if you knew what I found in the salon just now."

"What are you doing in the salon? It's nearly ten p.m."

There was a long sigh at the other end. "I've been working hard, Ivy. I care about this venture. A lot."

I glanced at Jilly and she raised I-told-you-so eyebrows.

"I know you do, Mom, and I think the salon's going to do great. It isn't safe to be there that late alone, though."

I expected an argument—a reminder that Clover Grove wasn't a den of iniquity like Boston. Instead there was a long pause. Maybe she was considering all the recent threats to my safety, to the farm and even the family. Not long ago they'd called a family meeting to ask me to sell the farm and take up a safer job in town. Luckily that dark cloud passed and no one mentioned it again. They seemed to accept the futility of asking me to give up my passion in life. Nothing would part me from my duty to my animals. It sounded like tempting fate to say that out loud too often, however, so I let stony silence speak for me.

"I shouldn't have come alone," Mom said. "You're absolutely right."

It wasn't often I heard those words from my mother. Dahlia Galloway was extremely confident in her own opinions, yet tonight, her voice sounded tentative.

"But you did, and now something's changed your mind," I prompted.

"I didn't intend to, but I was in the neighborhood. I had a date with a new gentleman from Dorset Hills." She picked up steam. "I use the term 'gentleman' loosely because he was anything but. First, he was late. Second, he was extremely handsy for a first date. And third, he expected me to go Dutch on the tab."

"Unspeakable." I grinned at Jilly. "Boot him from your rotation immediately, if not sooner."

"Ivy, have you been drinking?" Mom asked.

"No, but I was about to start. We have a nice bottle of wine here. So if you don't mind..."

"I do mind. I mind very much."

Now there was a distinct quaver in her voice. Dahlia Galloway didn't quaver. Ever. When my dad left her with six young kids to raise on her own, she didn't quaver. When one of us got into big trouble—usually Poppy—she didn't quaver. I bet she didn't even quaver while giving birth. Yet tonight, she was at her new salon quavering. Something was definitely wrong.

"Mom, tell me," I said, softening my tone. "You went to the salon, and then what happened?"

"I was just going to take some measurements for shelving. We're expecting a big shipment of product later in the week and there's no room upstairs. But when I opened the door to the basement, well..."

Her voice drifted off.

"What? You saw a mouse?"

"Worse." Her voice was muffled, as if she'd covered her mouth with her hand, or one of her many artful scarves. "Much worse."

"A rat?"

"Worse, Ivy. Much worse."

"A snake?"

"No, not a snake." Her voice quavered more. "That would be bad, though."

"Mom, just tell me. We could play this game all night."

"You need to come over. Right now."

"I am not coming over to deal with your vermin issue. That's why you added a son to your bouquet of daughters. Just because I'm a farmer doesn't mean I like dealing with pests."

"But you're an expert with—uh—problems like this."

"Problems like what?" There was a note of alarm in my voice and Jilly came over. Keats leaned into my right leg and Percy swished back and forth against my left.

"With... dead things. You'll know what to do. I know you will."

I started to pace across the tiles of the large kitchen. Jilly followed me, and Keats followed her, and Percy came last.

"Okay, now I'm officially worried, Mom. Tell me exactly what's died in the salon."

"It's so sad, darling. Tragic. I can't speak of it. Please come over right now."

I stopped walking and Jilly crashed into me from behind. "Are you... *crying*?"

There was a pause, as if she were checking. She'd taught all of her girls that crying betrayed weakness, and I became so accomplished at concealing my emotions people joked my tear ducts were stitched shut. Repression was an excellent skill for HR.

"Yes, I think I am crying." She sounded surprised. "Bring some tissues, darling."

I went to the door to collect my coat off a hook. "You have tissues. You're in a salon."

"Chintzy single ply that will make my eyes puff. I told Iris we need quality tissues." Her voice sounded a little stronger already. "Jilly, you wouldn't offer your guests anything less than a three-ply, would you?"

Jilly looked startled at being caught out eavesdropping on the conversation, but she rolled with it, as always. "Dahlia, I'll bring you the best tissues money can buy. What else do you need?"

"Thank you, sweetheart. You're such a dear." Mom sniffed loudly. "Bring the wine you were about to pour. I think we're all going to need it."

MOM WAS SITTING in her barber's chair in the darkness when I pressed my nose to the glass at Bloomers. She was so still and small that she looked barely more than a child. But when my eyes adjusted, I saw she held her phone in one hand and a straightedge razor in the other.

"What is going on?" I muttered, glancing from Jilly, who shrugged, down to Keats. The dog's ruff was up and his tail was down, which was the opposite of his normal demeanor when visiting Mom.

"She doesn't look too fussed," Jilly said, while I tapped gently on the glass. "I mean, other than the straightedge."

"I have a bad feeling about this," I said. "And Keats does, too. There's more to worry about here than a dead rat, I'm afraid."

"Oh no," Jilly said. "The last thing we all need is more trouble."

Mom's teeth showed as she slid out of the chair and walked across the salon. There was a hint of the usual spring in her step, as if she were on her own personal runway. I suppose she was, now. "On the other hand, she's sort of smiling. Maybe I'm just being paranoid."

"You don't think...?" There was a note of vague horror in Jilly's voice. "No. That's crazy."

"What?" I asked. "Are you worried about her date? The handsy cheapskate?"

My best friend nodded apologetically. "I'm sorry for even raising it."

"Don't be. I wondered the same thing. Maybe he followed her here and she... did something desperate."

"But then she wouldn't be smiling," Jilly said, as Mom unlatched the door. "Would she?"

"Mom works in mysterious ways. But so far, the only thing I've known her to kill is traffic signage and other obstacles in Buttercup's path."

The door cracked open and Mom beckoned us in with her phone, while the straightedge fell to her side and got swallowed in the folds of her A-line blue wool dress. The handsy cheapskate hadn't earned her signature red and never would.

"Girls, come in," she said. "Hurry. You, too, Keats."

Once we were inside, she locked the door behind us and then clicked briskly to the back of the salon. We followed in a single file—me, Jilly and then Keats—just as we had at home, only without Percy, who'd only upset Mom more.

"Mom, out with it. You've left us in suspense long enough. I could barely keep Buttercup on the road, I was so flustered."

"Buttercup can tell when you're distracted," Mom said. "The most belligerent car I ever owned. But we put up with so much for beauty, don't we?"

"Quit stalling, or I'm calling a family meeting on the spot and Daisy can deal with you."

"No!" The façade dropped away. "I don't want Daisy to know. I don't want *anyone* to know."

"Please tell me you didn't slash the handsy cheapskate," I said.

"What?" She turned to stare at me, and in the dim light at the rear of the salon, her hazel eyes were pools of darkness. "I didn't slash anyone, Ivy Rose. How could you even think such a thing?"

"Well, you were talking about dead things and you're holding a straightedge. Forgive me if I put two and two together and mentally murdered your bad date."

"My date was no gentleman, but as far as I know he's currently back in Dorset Hills with the dollars he saved."

I heaved a sigh of relief. "I'm sorry for jumping to conclusions like that. There's been so much trauma recently. Jilly and I both have PTSD."

"It's crazy how murder crosses our mind so readily now," Jilly said. The relief in her voice was obvious, too.

When I looked down at Keats, however, he was still very much on alert. His ears were forward, his ruff up, and his tail stuck straight out, like a bottlebrush. Normally that only happened when there was an imminent threat.

Mom started to walk again and I said, "Wait." I thought about reaching out and remembered the straightedge. One sudden move and my livestock could be orphaned. "Something is wrong here. Very wrong."

"I know, darling. That's what I was trying to tell you on the phone."

"Keats is worried. We're in danger."

Mom raised her blade. "Hence the weapon. But there's safety in numbers."

"Dahlia, please," Jilly said. "My heart can't handle this kind of stress anymore."

"I think you two can handle this better than anyone else," Mom said, flinging open the basement door. "Flashlights, please."

We all turned on our phone lights in the same instant and aimed them down the stairs. At the bottom someone lay face down in such an awkward position that I knew it was her final resting place even before I saw the gold-handled scissors sticking out of her back.

"Oh no." My voice was raspy and barely more than a whisper. "You stabbed Portia Parson."

CHAPTER NINE

M om turned on me so fast her light blinded me. "I did no such thing. How dare you suggest I am capable of murder? Again! Once was insulting enough, Ivy."

"This is the third time, actually," I said. "Because you keep threatening people."

"I set boundaries, that's all."

"Well, you set a big boundary with Portia and now she's dead in your salon. Did she come back to get her haircut evened out and fall backward onto your scissors? That would have been a spectacular move."

"Worthy of an Olympic gymnast," Jilly whispered.

Keats mumbled something and I looked down at him. His ruff had settled and his tail was at half mast. Whatever the threat, it had passed.

"I have no idea how this happened," Mom said. "And for the record, our scissors are just where we left them." She gestured to the two workstations. "Someone came armed, apparently."

"What did you do after you found Portia?" I asked.

"Like I told you, I came in to measure for shelving. Nothing at all seemed amiss so I moved some boxes around and cleaned for a bit. Then I opened the basement door, flicked on the light and saw... that."

"Then what did you do?" I asked.

"I turned off all the lights and huddled by the door with my straightedge. Then I called you."

"Mom, the murderer could still be downstairs. Didn't you call 911?"

"There's no one here," she said. "Look at Keats."

Even my mom was relying on my dog to assess our safety.

"But there could have been then. And instead, you called me and placed a special order for deluxe tissues."

She waved one manicured hand. "People react to stress in strange ways. It was clear to me that nothing could be done for Portia by that point. Is it so terrible I wanted you by my side when I confronted this issue?"

"Wouldn't your police officer son be the better candidate for this particular job?"

"Not when you're the expert in being wrongly accused of murder," she said. "And I'm quite sure that Kellan Harper will do just that when you call him. I want you to use your skills to handle him."

I signalled Jilly to call 911 and turned to stare at my mother. "What skills would those be?"

"It's a curious mix of human resources and detective work, I suppose," Mom said. "I have no idea where you got them." Her smile finally reappeared. "Also, you have influence over Chief Harper."

"I can't stand in the way of him doing his job, Mom."

She waved again. "Please. You do that all the time. Now you need to do it for me. And for Portia. Whatever her shortcomings—and she had plenty—she didn't deserve to end up down there." She gestured to the stairwell with her straightedge. "Like that."

"Put that thing down right now before someone else gets hurt," I said. "Like Jilly, Keats or me."

"Of course."

She didn't move, which confirmed my suspicion that she was in shock. "Come and sit down, Mom."

"I—I don't think I can. I'm feeling..." Her voice drifted off. Mom had never been terribly in tune with her feelings and now she couldn't put her finger on exactly what was roiling inside.

"Scared?"

"Maybe. Yes, I suppose so. That makes sense, doesn't it?"

"It most certainly does." I carefully pried her fingers off the straightedge. "I've never seen you so rattled. You're probably in shock."

"Whoever killed Portia may have been after *me*, Ivy."

I carried the blade with two hands as Jilly guided Mom over to the barber chair and eased her into it. It took a pretty firm push to get her seated again. Once she was down, Keats rested his long muzzle on her lap, angled slightly to give her the full benefit of his sympathetic brown eye. His tail fanned gently for the first time since she'd called earlier. Mom's fingers dropped to his ears and almost instantly her breath evened out.

"I doubt anyone was after you," I said. "You have your share of detractors, but I'm sure Portia has far more. And no one could have mistaken her for you. She's twice your size."

"True." Her voice sounded stronger. "And that dreadful hair."

"Made more dreadful by her interrupted haircut after you threatened her."

She glared at me. "Talk like that isn't going to get me the justice I deserve, Ivy. This is my salon and Portia was in here after hours. She obviously had her own key because the door was locked when I got here."

"And either someone else had a key, too, or she made poor choices in the company she kept tonight," I said. "I assume the killer had already left through the back door when you arrived."

Sirens blared nearby and Mom reached out to squeeze my hand. "You believe me, don't you? That I didn't do this?"

I looked down at her. Never had she looked smaller, or, truthfully, older. She'd fended off aging with fierce determination and plenty of product, but tonight she'd put on 20 years.

As rash as Mom could be, however, I knew she wasn't a murderer. This was a case of wrong place, wrong time, and I knew exactly what that felt like.

"I do believe you," I said, squeezing back.

"Me too," Jilly said. "We've got your back, Dahlia."

"And so does Keats," I said, pointing to the tuft of his white tail, still fanning. "He knows you're innocent. I've seen him with people who aren't, remember?"

"That *is* reassuring," she said. "If only the chief would accept Keats as a character witness."

"He does," I said. "At least sometimes."

"This is going to be so awkward," she said. "Just when things were finally looking up for me. I love this salon. What if I lose it?"

I walked to the door, flicked on all the lights and twisted the lock to let the police in. "One thing I've learned the hard way is that the truth always comes out eventually. And I hope for everyone's sake that this is an open and shut case."

The small salon filled quickly with uniformed officers, including Kellan and my brother. No matter the circumstances, Asher couldn't help lighting up when he saw Jilly. It was involuntary, like a tic. He was a happy-go-lucky person by nature, who'd ended up on the police force after a short stint as a fitness trainer. Sometimes I wondered if he regretted the career change, because fixing flabby abs was the least of his worries now. His smile was always at the ready but never more so than when my best friend was in the room. It was love at first sight for Asher, but Jilly was methodical and deliberate about everything from head-hunting to cooking. She'd take her sweet time about making up her mind and Asher would have to cool his jets.

Kellan, on the other hand, had the demeanor of a big city police chief, not to mention movie star looks. I bet more than a few female criminals were happy to be detained, just to spend a little time in the interrogation room with him. I knew the room well from a couple of intense chats. Mom did, too, and the way she squared her shoulders now suggested she was preparing mentally.

"Chief Harper," she said, pleasantly. "I'm sorry we have to meet in such circumstances. You must understand I'm in shock over what happened to Portia Parson on my premises. Ivy said she's never seen me so rattled."

"Mom, just let Kellan—I mean Chief Harper—ask the questions, okay? It works better that way."

"It most certainly does," Kellan said. His tone told me to stand down. My boyfriend was off duty, and with another Galloway murder problem, perhaps he'd stay that way permanently.

"I'm just worried you'll see what happened here and jump to the wrong conclusions," Mom said.

"I never jump to conclusions, Mrs. Galloway," he said, before turning to head downstairs. "Have a seat, ladies. This is going to take a while." He turned at the top of the stairs. "Ivy, the dog's eying me like a stuffed toy. This isn't the time for his games."

I looked down at Keats and saw his mouth hanging open in a sloppy smile. "He heard you. Your pant cuffs are safe tonight."

"They'd better be." The faintest hint of a smile played on his lips, which I found reassuring. My boyfriend wasn't far beneath the surface of official propriety.

After the entire team disappeared downstairs, Mom said, "I hope he remembers that later."

"Remembers what?" I asked.

"How much he likes you. It would be inconvenient to have his future mother-in-law in jail."

"Mom! Don't say things like that."

"Let me rephrase it." She crossed her legs in the barber chair, clearly recovering her mojo. "You wouldn't marry Chief Hottie if he put me in jail, would you?"

I looked quickly at the basement door to make sure Kellan was truly gone. He was... and so was Keats. The dog had clearly followed the police downstairs, either to annoy Kellan, or do his own investigating.

"It would depend on whether or not you were guilty," I told Mom.

"You've already said you know I'm not."

I shrugged again. "Keats believes you so I'm giving you the benefit of the doubt. But it's up to Kellan to make the case. He's very good at his job, Mom. He didn't get to be the youngest chief of police in the state by letting emotions cloud his judgement."

Mom turned to Jilly. "You won't desert me in my hour of need, will you? We'll be family soon, too."

Jilly's face flushed bright red. "Ivy already calls me family, Dahlia. I love being an honorary Galloway."

"Wonderful. Then maybe you can convince my daughter to put me first and use her powers of investigation to clear my name and the salon. That's what you three do, isn't it?" She made a circle with her index finger that included Keats, in his absence. "Solve crimes?"

"Not by choice," I said. "Necessity keeps demanding it because it's involved the farm. This time is different. And remember... you asked me to get out of the crime business."

"Because it was bringing trouble on the family. And now look what's happened. You got into a situation with Portia and I defended you and now she's died with a terrible haircut that reflects very poorly on Iris' skills."

I turned to Jilly. "Lord, give me strength. She's saying this is my fault."

"Is she right?" The deep voice belonged to Chief Harper, not boyfriend Kellan. He was in the basement doorway with Keats at his side.

"No, she's not right. How could you say that?"

He cued something up on his phone and handed it to me. Jilly crowded closer and we saw an image of someone crouched in front of the old Bingham manor, peering into the dining room window.

"What have you to say about that?" he asked. "Portia sent me the photo yesterday. Apparently she was out walking on the grounds and saw some creeping Ivy."

"You can't prove that's me," I said, trying to hand the phone back.

"Blow it up," he said. "The dog and the cat are a give-away. I heard Jilly was in the getaway golf cart."

"Okay, fine. Sue me for wanting to know where Edna's missing cats had gone. They're over there now, along with plenty of others. You and your team need to save them all."

His eyebrows shot up as he processed that new information. "After we've been through the manor I'll call Animal Services."

"Animal services! Edna should have the right to place the cats as she likes."

"Well, I can't just open the door and release them all, hoping they'll run miles back to Edna's. Some of them aren't feral. How would they survive?"

"I'll deal with it, Kellan. I can take responsibility for them until Edna gets home." I was pleading with him now. "Once they're in the pound, I'll never get them out. It would be against County bylaws to let me take more than six. What if the County...?"

He rested his hand on my shoulder for a second, letting the boyfriend surface. "I'll speak to them. Go home and stay safe. My first priority is Portia right now."

Jilly gave me a little smile. "You can adopt six, and Edna can adopt six and we can round up some other friends, right? Like Teri Mason and Mandy McCain. With enough friends, we could get them all out of jail."

"Right," I said, catching her drift. "Well, if that's how it has to be, Kellan, I understand."

His eyes narrowed suspiciously. "It'll take us a few days to finish our investigation here and at the manor. No running around on harebrained stunts. I shouldn't need to remind you of this, but I probably do... there's a killer on the loose."

Mom's smile had returned, appreciating that the spotlight was on me instead of her. "Girls, what have I told you about sneaking around at night?"

Kellan turned to her. "Probably the same thing she told you when she heard you were here tonight. Now get your things, Mrs. Galloway, and let's head down to the station."

Mom started to protest, but Keats did the arguing for her. He darted at Kellan's pant legs and tried to drive him away.

"Keats, off," I said. "Kellan's just doing his job. Let's go home and do ours. We have livestock to protect."

Kellan gently nudged the dog away with one boot. "You do that. I'll be in touch tomorrow, ladies."

"I look forward to it," I said, snapping my fingers at the dog. "Please ask Officer Galloway to see his mother home safely when you're done, will you?"

CHAPTER TEN

Miss Bingham was dressed impeccably when I dropped in unannounced at Sunny Acres retirement villa the next morning. In Clover Grove, it was still common practice to visit without calling ahead. Personally, I hated being on the receiving end of those visits, but making them worked in my favor quite often. It was my first time doing so at a seniors' residence, however, and my conscience did light up with guilty fireworks. Luckily, the smile on Miss Bingham's face told me I was welcome.

"Why, Ivy Galloway, what a pleasure to see you," she said, coming into the foyer after the concierge buzzed her room. "And your handsome young friend in his tuxedo. Where's my ginger admirer, Percy?"

"He wanted to join us, trust me," I said. "It's so hard to escape without him. I need to factor an extra half hour into every plan just to round him up and trap him. He expects equal rights with the dog."

"Well, he is the most dog-like cat I've met," she said, leading me away from the concierge toward the front door. "How about we take a turn in the courtyard? It will be more private." Lowering her voice, she added, "Sunny Acres is full of nosy parkers and I don't want to give people any more to talk about than they already have."

I laughed as I helped her into her coat. "Why would they talk about you?"

There were a few wheeled walkers lined up in a corner. She gestured for me to grab one, and then passed me her cane.

"I'm too proud to use a walker when I'm in town," she said. "But here I still look pretty spry compared to most people. That's one thing they talk about. Some think I'm not sick enough to be here. But I simply couldn't keep up the manor anymore and it was falling to ruin around me. So what they talk about most is what I did with my property."

I opened the door and she glided through in front of me pushing the walker. "You mean selling it to Portia Parson?" I asked.

"Exactly. Everyone said it should have stayed in the family." She shook her head. "My own family didn't want it. I offered to sell it to my nephew, Michael, years ago so I could downsize before I actually needed to. He didn't want to move home to Clover Grove. So I found someone who'd love it and care for it like a pet."

I swallowed hard at that. She clearly had no idea what had become of her stately home.

We walked around the side of the villa and followed a smooth, paved path lined with trees and some hearty asters. The U-shaped building provided enough shelter to keep things flourishing longer than elsewhere. It fit the retirement theme perfectly.

Benches dotted the courtyard and I pointed to the first one. "Could we sit down for a moment, Miss Bingham? There's something I need to tell you."

"No need to stop just yet," she said, pushing ahead with her walker. "I already know about what happened to Portia, if that's what you're worried about."

"You do?" I'd skipped half my morning chores to get here early, figuring the notorious Clover Grove grapevine probably wasn't hardwired into the retirement community.

"This place thrives on gossip, as I said. Your handsome boyfriend probably hadn't even closed the squad car door on your mother before someone came to tell me about it. I was already in bed, mind you, but I got up to wait with everyone else for news. It wasn't clear for some time who'd passed away, and as you can imagine, there was no sleep for me after that."

Keats kept a steady pace at her side, looking up frequently with his brown eye. She managed a smile when she noticed, and he swished the white tuft of his tail in response.

"I'm so sorry," I said, simply. "I know how close you two were."

"We were," Miss Bingham said. "At least at one time. Less so recently."

"Oh? What changed?"

She gave a slight shrug, keeping a tight grip on the walker. "Honestly, I'm not quite sure. Portia was always a little quirky, as you probably know. She had rules for cat care that clients were expected to follow, even when she wasn't cat-sitting. There were approved foods, an approved schedule, approved veterinary care and approved codes of cat conduct. She didn't endorse single cat households, for example, and refused to work for people if you didn't meet her expectations."

"That's a strong stance for a small business."

"It grated on some people, no question, because she was

also the most reliable service in town. I didn't mind, because I knew her heart was in the right place. You know as well as I do that passionate animal people get strange notions, sometimes."

"Yeah," I said, grinning. "I'm one of them. But someone must have taken serious issue with Portia's attitude."

Pausing, Miss Bingham peered at me over her glasses. "You're sure it wasn't your mother? Dahlia can be a pistol, too."

"No argument there," I said. "But Mom's all talk and no action. Besides, she's madly in love with her new salon and now it's in jeopardy."

"I can't imagine why Portia was there after hours, other than to confront your mother."

"So late in the evening? It seems odd she'd come by then."

Miss Bingham started walking again. "Well, a clash like she had with Dahlia wasn't unusual for Portia. It was just the most recent."

I looked up at the villa and was startled to see so many gray or bald heads in the windows. No one was even pretending not to spy on us.

"I would imagine the police will come by today to talk to you," I said. "But I want you to know that I'm also committed to figuring out what happened to Portia."

Turning, she waggled her iron gray eyebrows. "And how will your handsome boyfriend feel about that?"

"About as you'd expect," I said, laughing. "Jilly says he's equal parts infuriated and infatuated."

"Sounds like the perfect balance," she said. "You need to keep them off balance and on their toes, Ivy. Just because I never married doesn't mean I don't know a thing or two about men."

I had no doubt. Not only was she still attractive in her eighties, she had a lovely voice, a pleasant manner and a sharp wit.

"Why didn't you marry?" I asked. "I bet you could have had your choice among Clover Grove's eligible men."

"Still could." She tipped her head at the peeping residents. "I have a suitor or two. But I never found the right man and wouldn't settle for less." Finally she gestured to a bench near a fountain that still burbled. "There aren't enough good men in this town. They all run off to chase careers and end up marrying city girls. Not that I have any complaints about Caroline, my nephew's wife. She's as meek as they come and quite talented with crafts. I've never heard her say a harsh word about anyone. Still, there are so many lovely, spirited women here with limited choices, like your sisters." She eased down on the bench and looked up at me. "Not you, though. You don't have to settle, and I'm happy for you."

My face got a little steamy as it always did when Kellan came up. Even with the "boyfriend" word getting tossed around it would be quite a while before I felt comfortable discussing it.

"I take it Portia never married?"

Miss Bingham shook her head. "Hard to say whether she was too quirky to find love, or whether not finding it *made* her quirky. Unlike me, she was a little bitter about being single."

"Maybe there was a story. A heartbreak in her past. That's what happened to someone else I know."

"Edna Evans, I presume?" She laughed at my expression. "I've been around this town even longer than Edna, remember? We were friends once, before she got..."

"Quirky?" I offered.

"Downright strange, in her case. I do hear she's mellowed since you came into her life."

"Credit goes to the feral cat colony she adopted," I said. "And that's really what caused tension between Portia and my mom. Although Mom doesn't know it."

She patted the seat beside her with her right hand and offered her left hand to Keats, who happily submitted to being stroked with sapphires, diamonds and emeralds. "Please elaborate."

I told her about the missing cats, and my suspicion Portia had been pilfering them. Her eyes brightened as I described my joyride through the trails with Jilly to the old manor.

"Keats and Percy came with us," I said. "We peeked into the dining room window of your old home."

"And...?"

"And I saw that Portia had added quite a few cats to the six you left her."

"How many more?" Now her voice became quietly thunderous.

"Enough to be called a cat hoarder," I said. "Although I'm really not one to judge since I'm always taking on more rescues, just like Hannah Pemberton."

"Ivy. How many?"

I couldn't avoid the direct question. "Dozens."

"Dozens? Plural?"

"I'm afraid so, yes."

"Inside the house? All of them?"

"That's a good question. There may be some outdoors as well. But there were dozens inside."

"Inside my mother's stately dining room? The one that hosted two governors and many other dignitaries?"

"It was a lovely table," I said. "I couldn't help but notice it, although I didn't stay long."

"An Arthur Leemington original that my grandfather commissioned for my grandmother as a wedding gift. Are you suggesting the cats were on that table?"

Scuffing the smattering of dry leaves on the path with my boot, I nodded and mumbled another apology. "There were just so darn many there was probably no place they *didn't* go."

Miss Bingham's hand dropped away from Keats and she stared into space. "If I'd known that, well... It's best I didn't or perhaps I'd be a suspect in the murder, too. Portia and I had an agreement that she'd keep the place exactly as it was till I passed. That way I could go over now and then and remember days past."

"When was the last time you were there?" I asked.

"Six months ago, give or take. Everything was fine then. There were my six cats and two she'd brought with her, which was reasonable. I kept asking to visit and she kept making excuses. Now I know why."

"I have friends who knew Portia and they said she'd seemed stressed lately."

Her lips sealed up tight and we sat in silence for a few moments. Finally, Keats shoved his head under her hand none too subtly and she took the hint. A few minutes of stroking his ears did the trick and her lips parted again. "I was worried about her. In fact, I often thought about taking a cab over there to see what was going on. But I never did. Maybe part of me knew something had gone far wrong but was afraid to ask. Once you're in here—" she waved her free hand at the facility behind her— "you start to feel helpless. Like you can't function in the real world anymore. That's the real curse of places like these. Not the loneliness or the gossip."

The pain in her voice reverberated in my chest. I knew those feelings all too well. For the two years before Keats broke me out of my corporate cage, they were my constant companions. I looked down at him now and saw he'd repositioned himself so that we could both pat him. My busy, driven dog was turning into a therapy dog after all. He was mellowing with maturity, like the best of us.

"I'm sure there was nothing you could have done," I said. "Sometimes life gets overwhelming. Some people eat or drink too much, others shop too much. Portia collected too many cats under one roof."

Miss Bingham nodded. "Money was tight, I know that. She was always coming to me for more. After selling the house to her I gave her a small allowance to keep it up. I assumed she was making repairs, like she told me."

"The house needs work, I could see that. But keeping so many cats healthy would cost a lot. I know what I pay in vet bills."

She shook her head over and over. "This is most unfortunate, Ivy, and there's little I can do from here. Please tell me you'll look into it."

"I'll do what I can, Miss Bingham."

"Hazel," she said, reaching for my hand. "We're friends now, I hope."

"It's an honor," I said. "I'd love to have you out to the farm to take the grand tour and enjoy one of Jilly's scrumptious meals."

"I'd like that very much. Then I can see that beautiful marmalade Percy, again."

"Just give me a day or two to poke around before Kellan figures out what I'm doing."

Her laugh sounded like it belonged to a woman half her age. "Don't annoy one of the few good men left in Clover Grove, Ivy. You'll need to be very stealthy. Can you do it?"

I pointed to Keats. Sensing the shift in the mood, he'd left us to stalk a tame and chubby squirrel that had likely been stuffed with nuts by the residents. The dog advanced so gradually the squirrel didn't notice. Just before he made his last lunge, I called him off. Far from being disappointed, his tail was high and his ears pricked. It was all about fun. He didn't even want to catch it.

"Keats is my role model for stealth," I told Hazel now. "Percy's got flair, too."

"You could do worse," she said, laughing again. "Please keep me posted. If I were you, my first stop would be Chez Belle on Main Street. Portia argued with the owner recently over cat protocol, and it led to the usual mudslinging on both sides. It seemed like Belle took it more seriously than strictly necessary."

"I can imagine why. Portia didn't play nice, Hazel. Remember, she threatened to start an online petition to get my farm shut down. Later she said she'd post terrible reviews of Bloomers. If Belle heard something similar, she might react strongly."

Hazel pushed herself up off the bench, refusing the hand I held out. "I'm afraid Portia was losing her way. She had a run-in with the organic butcher. And even the Langman sisters, I believe. But she was very kind to me over the years and I truly regret missing the signs."

"I'll pay Belle a visit," I said, as we started back. Keats frisked around us, sending up swirls of leaves like a carefree puppy. Maybe being off the farm lifted the load of responsibility because I didn't often see him play like that. "Would you mind if I asked something personal?"

"We're friends, now," she said, stopping to give me her full attention.

"Do you know who stood to inherit the manor from Portia?"

"Ah." She gave me a sly smile. "I have a good lawyer, Ivy. The house reverts to me since I'm still on the right side of the grass. What I'll do with it now, I don't know. Michael still doesn't want to come home. He's got itchy feet."

"Don't worry. In the short term, we can hire a reliable caretaker. My farm manager, Charlie, will know someone."

"Of course, Charlie. Is he still dating your mother?"

The Sunny Acres grapevine *was* quite good. "I'm not sure," I said. "I have a 'don't ask don't tell' policy about Mom's dating life. It's hard enough keeping up with her minor vendettas."

"Like I said, Dahlia's a pistol."

"But not a murderer," I said. "I'm quite sure if we put our heads together we can figure out exactly who made The Cat Lady sing."

Hazel smiled at my joke and the last vestiges of the old ache in my chest loosened up and blew away like the leaves. As Hazel bent to plant a kiss squarely between Keats' ears, I hoped she felt the same way.

CHAPTER ELEVEN

I glanced over at Keats as we drove from Sunny Acres to Daisy's house. Jilly had woken with a headache, which wasn't surprising after the grizzly discovery in Bloomers the night before. She'd turned down my invitation to attend a Galloway family meeting, well aware that these gatherings were a recipe for a full-on migraine.

Family meetings were almost always about bad news. We were all busy, so no one ever suggested getting together if a simple text or phone call would do the job. That meant most of our get-togethers were emergency interventions, not unlike the Rescue Mafia's 911s. One upside of living in Boston had been getting a free pass on most of them. Now I was paying a price. Somehow, since my homecoming, I'd ended up picking up the mediator torch from Daisy, who was justifiably exhausted from corralling Mom and our siblings.

"I'm glad you're with me, buddy," I said, as Keats braced himself against the dashboard. "Mom, at least, will make this about me and the trouble I've brought to the family since buying Runaway Farm."

Keats mumbled something that sounded appropriately sympathetic. It probably cost him a little because he actually loved visiting Daisy's house. That had less to do with seeing the family than with my twin nephews' twin ferrets, who were rarely caged, much to Daisy's dismay. Despite slinking and stalking on both sides, they must have reached a mutual understanding because no one got hurt.

"I hope you didn't spend all your empathy at Sunny Acres," I said. "I was super impressed, by the way. You outdid Remi's beagle, Leo, back there. I already thought you were pretty much perfect but you've transcended my expectations yet again."

His next vocalization sounded like a humblebrag.

"Go ahead and swagger. You earned it. Without you, Hazel may have been too upset to help. Now we can start trying to vindicate Mom and do the right thing by Portia."

The dog looked over at me with his cool blue eye and his message didn't need mumble-captions.

"Oh, I know. Portia was mean and could have caused a world of trouble for the farm. But something tells me she didn't deserve what happened. Clearing Mom's name will likely flush out some clues for the police. We've got to play this one safe, okay? I don't want to derail things with Kellan. Besides, you and I have had enough near-death experiences to last awhile."

He gave a noncommittal rumble. Either he didn't believe me, or he didn't want to play it safe. As sweet as he'd been with Hazel this morning, I knew he'd rather be deployed as a field agent.

Mom and my sisters were already in their usual places in Daisy's kitchen when I arrived. Asher was pulling a double shift as he and his colleagues picked over the salon with a fine-tooth comb. It was just as well. Our discussion was sure to put him in an awkward position. He didn't want to be caught between Kellan and me, or between Kellan and Mom for that matter. Asher just wanted everyone to agree, and that wasn't how the justice system worked.

"Ivy, I'm so glad you're here," Mom said. "Your sisters have been ganging up on me and I need someone on my side."

Everyone laughed. In our family, I was named least likely to side with Mom. She must be desperate to pretend that was even possible.

"I'll see you get a fair trial before the family tribunal," I said, tossing my coat on the pile in the front hall and then taking my spot at the kitchen table.

Mom was as dressed down as I'd ever seen her, in a pair of harem-style pants and a baggy tunic. It was like she wanted to be swallowed up in clothes so no one recognized her. Her hair was limp and her lips bare. She still wore a touch of powder and mascara, but otherwise looked like the average midlifer next door. It spoke volumes about her state of mind.

Normally Daisy spent much of a family meeting trying to grab a white china mug from Mom's clutches to scrape red, waxy lipstick off the rim. Today, the cup was unmarked, which lightened the load for my clean-freak sister. She filled the void by using a small brush to clean the grout in the tiles behind the sink.

Iris looked much the worse for wear as well. She was still in plaid flannel pajamas with an oversized sweater that had capacity to warm us all. I wondered if she'd driven over in bedroom slippers or borrowed them from Daisy.

Perhaps sensing a rare opportunity to outshine Mom, Poppy had taken things to the other extreme. As the wild child of the family even at 36, Poppy dyed her hair bright colors often and when she had time on her hands, combined them. Her current coiffure alternated streaks of blue, red, pink and orange, which clashed with a short green McInnis tartan kilt. To my knowledge, we had no Scottish blood.

Violet and Daisy were both dressed in black, which was unusual. Perhaps it was meant to be a sign of respect for either the dead Cat Lady, or the moribund salon.

"There won't be a trial of any sort," Mom said, struggling to stay upright on the stool at the counter. It was a challenge at any time, given her petite stature, but the slippery harem pants made it worse. Finally she managed to hook the heels of sensible flats over the top rung and gripped the counter with her fingers. "Where's Jilly when I need her?"

"She has a terrible headache. Is it any surprise?" I slouched in my seat. "Jilly left a successful and sedate life to help me launch this inn and it seems like there's never-ending drama."

"It wasn't like this until *you* came home," Mom said.

"Mom!" The chorus sounded like all four sisters.

I looked down at Keats. "Told you she'd blame me. I thought she'd at least wait till I had a coffee."

Daisy pulled down another white mug and filled it to the brim, knowing I'd forfeit cream in favor of caffeine. "You may need to cut Mom a little slack today, Ivy. You can see she's not herself."

"I certainly can. Who is this strange woman wearing genie pants and why is she at our family meeting? More importantly, can I get three wishes?"

"They're not genie pants, thank you very much, but even I need to be comfortable sometimes. Especially after the brutal grilling I got from your boyfriend last night."

"Boyfriend?" This time only Poppy, Iris and Violet

chimed in. Daisy already knew Kellan had formalized our status. She was the only family member I confided in, but if she let things slip with Mom like that, I'd downgrade her to the sister bush-leagues without a moment's regret. Jilly and Keats were the only confidantes I needed.

"Things are going okay with Kellan," I said. "Which is why I don't really want to rock the boat with too much sleuthing."

Mom's glare was less fearsome without full makeup. "This isn't the time to gain common sense, Ivy. My reputation is at stake."

"And the salon's reputation," Iris added. "It's an uphill battle to start any business but who can indulge and relax when someone died in the basement? With my shears in her back?"

"I predict it will be busier than ever once you're cleared to reopen," I said. "I don't need to tell you how much people love gossip around here. In fact, I bet they book in pairs because they're both curious and nervous."

Iris brightened a little at the thought. "I hope you're right. Murders haven't done your inn any good, though."

"It's only been a couple of weeks since the last one." I shook my head at how crazy that sounded. "Things will pick up. I just need a few good guests to get back on track. My challenge is that locals don't need to use an inn, whereas everyone needs a haircut. They'll have to drive out of town to avoid you."

Iris straightened out of a hunch. "Good point. The people who can't drive will be back first."

"Then you offer a little incentive," I said. "Buy a haircut, get a manicure free or some such."

"Yes!" She looked more like her old self, and the rest of my sisters smiled too.

Mom shrugged. "I'm sure my gentlemen clients won't be as sensitive as the ladies. In fact, I've already had calls to rebook after cancelling my appointments. But when will the chief let us open again?"

I shrugged. "When he's explored every nook and cranny, and satisfied himself you're not a threat to society. No telling how long that will take. It's too bad you didn't stay a little longer with the handsy cheapskate to have an alibi. Iris is covered."

"Covered but fretting," Iris said. "I can't bear standing around to watch our debt build."

"Who said anything about standing around?" I asked. "We've got investigating to do."

"You said you were playing it safe," Daisy said. "Investigating doesn't sound very safe. Not when there's a murderer at large."

"Our definitions might differ. To me, 'safe' means making sure I have my butt covered if Kellan asks what I'm doing. And today, I'm going dress shopping with my family."

"Shopping!" The word echoed around the kitchen.

"What kind of dress?" Daisy's eyes had widened. "A wedding dress?"

"Oh, good lord, no. We've only had a few dates."

"What then?" She pointed at me with her grout brush. "You hate dresses."

"I need to replace the dress I borrowed from Jilly for the salon launch. Turns out llama spit stains are forever. Plus, we should find something spectacular for Mom and Iris to wear at the reopening party."

Iris looked appalled. "Another party?"

"Nothing screams innocence like a party and a nice

dress, am I right?" I said. "Maybe I should do that at the inn, too."

Mom slid off the stool. "There are two secondhand stores I've been dying to check out over in Fairbrook. Combing the racks with all of my daughters would help me recover from this horrible shock faster."

"Great idea," I said. "Let's get moving, ladies."

Keats strutted ahead of me to the door while my sisters called out protests behind me.

"We need to swing by my place," Mom said. She was plucking at her harem pants when I turned. "I can't go shopping like this. What will people think?"

"That you're incognito?" I suggested. "That's not a bad thing today, Mom. But time is of the essence on this particular mission. You can all carpool in Daisy's van and follow Buttercup down the yellow brick road."

CHAPTER TWELVE

M om put on flat-shoed brakes outside Chez Belle and when I grabbed her shoulders, started fighting like a wolverine.

"I am not going in there. Belle Tremblay and I don't see eye to eye on things."

"Why doesn't that surprise me?" I restrained her without breaking a sweat. Her thrashing might have foiled me in my pasty executive days, but now that I had pipes, it was easy enough to propel her through the door Daisy opened.

"I sure hope there's a good reason for this," Iris said. "Because I've never hit a designer shop in flannel pajamas before."

"Good call on borrowing sneakers," I said. "Bedroom slippers never do a dress justice."

"Like you would know," Iris said, managing a grin.

"Jilly said so. She knows."

Iris had perked up like a flower after rain and I was impressed by her resilience. Normally, you couldn't keep a

Galloway down for long. My previous career had stolen that capacity from me, but it was back in spades.

I kept a firm grip on Mom as we packed into the store. When she deliberately let her legs give out, I practically carried her. She was as light as a bird, although the baggy fabrics made things awkward.

"This is fun," Poppy said. "I think I'm going to like sleuthing."

"Poppy? First rule of investigation is silence," I said. "Act normal."

"In normal life I'd never darken the door of this place." She tossed her rainbow of hair. "It gives me the creeps."

"Shut it, you," I said as Mom nearly slithered out of my grip. "We're here as a family to buy dresses. That's our cover story. You and Mom are superb actors, so I suggest you find your inner thespian."

"I resent that," Mom said. However, she stopped squirming the very second the store owner emerged from the back room. Her shoulders went back and she stood a little taller, as if imagining high heels, a red dress and a full face of makeup.

"Whereas I'm flattered," Poppy said, walking over to greet the owner. "Nice to see you again, Belle. We're here to try on some dresses for a special occasion. Can you handle the Galloway Five?"

Belle was an elegant woman of about Mom's age, and equally attractive in a different way. Her hair was fair and backcombed into an elaborate twist and she wore a flowy, floral dress that looked like perpetual summer. Scanning the circle, she stopped counting when she reached Mom.

"I can most definitely handle five," she said. "Six may put me over the top."

"Don't worry," I said. "Mom is excited to be here. She's always wanted one of your dresses and this is her chance."

Belle's carefully drawn eyebrows rose in a delicate dance as she eyed Mom's outfit. "How wonderful."

Mom flushed an odd shade of puce. She took pride in refurbishing used clothing to suit her trim style, and Belle's line of feminine frocks—many with layers of chiffon—offended her sensibilities. Worse, being seen here at less than her best made her the one-down in a dispute that appeared to be ongoing. Perhaps two or even three down, judging by the smirk on Belle's face. Then the designer's eyes dropped to Keats, who had leaned into my mom's leg to offer support, and the smirk faded.

Before she could complain, I raised my hand. "Keats is a therapy dog. I have the paperwork if you need to see it."

She chewed on that for a moment and seemed to swallow whatever she'd intended to say. "Ladies, tell me the occasion and let's get started, shall we?"

I stepped forward, surrendering custody of Mom to Daisy. "We're having another party at Bloomers and we all want to look our very best."

"A party?" The stenciled eyebrows swooped up again. "There was yellow hazard tape around the salon when I passed this morning."

"Temporary," I said. "It will reopen in no time and we want to be dressed for it. Nothing too showy, mind you."

"I should think not," Belle murmured. "Poor Portia."

Mom's color deepened but Iris and Daisy had her flanked in a human vise. With Violet behind, there was no escape.

"Poor Portia," I echoed. "It was a tragedy and we're all reeling. It's a Galloway tradition to gather as a family in times of need and do something positive. After this, we're going to visit cat rescues to contribute in Portia's memory." I glanced at Mom. "One of the best is in Fairbrook."

Releasing a sigh of resignation, Mom said, "Belle, I'd love to try on one of your creations. Something understated."

"Understated?" Belle said. "Red is your signature color. What you did with that dress of mine was... remarkable."

Ah. So Belle was miffed Mom had found one of her designs in a vintage shop and worked her dubious magic with a sewing machine.

"I'm sure she did her best to honor the original design," I said. "And your dress had a new life after someone else retired it."

"There was no honor involved in cutting off the skirt and replacing it entirely," Belle said. "There is no honor in red dye."

"It was stained!" Mom's voice notched up. "And chiffon has never been my friend. I'm so petite I look like a collectible doll."

Now Belle flushed. This battle wasn't going to end today, if ever. The best I could do was relegate Mom to my sisters and keep Belle distracted.

I signaled to Keats to stick with the others and led Belle to the racks of dresses that really were far too precious for any Galloway girl. With the exception of Mom and Poppy, we were all sensible to the core. Even Iris, the most stylish among us, liked clean lines. No fuss, no muss.

With Belle's help, I chose five different dresses—the simplest on the rack—and delivered them to my family, and then came back out front.

"I'm sorry about my mom," I whispered. "She's quite overcome by what happened."

"Of course," Belle said. "What a shock it must have been. I assume Portia came to the salon after hours to correct that horrible haircut. It looked like someone took a chainsaw to it." She covered her mouth. "Sorry. How tactless of me."

"It's all right," I said. "I'm sure every store owner in town is rattled today. If it could happen in Bloomers, it could happen anywhere."

That gave Belle pause. "I can't see how. It seems like a very isolated event. Dahlia and Portia had a very public disagreement, as I understand it."

"Over my work with animals, I'm afraid. Portia threatened me with bodily harm, which any mother would need to defend. There were witnesses."

"I heard Dahlia pulled a switchblade on Portia, right there in the salon. There were witnesses."

Just as I was about to blurt something caustic, a warm body pressed against my shin. Keats gave me the strength to force a smile instead. "Mom happened to be holding a straightedge razor when Portia threatened to shoot me, not to mention Keats and my friend Jilly. She was in the middle of shaving Wayne Flagg. There was no risk to Portia and I'm sure he'll verify that."

"Still, it's all very strange," Belle said.

"True, but Portia had a habit of rubbing people the wrong way. I heard you had an altercation with her, too."

Color soared up from the collar of her dress and she grabbed her throat as if to stop it. "Who told you that?"

"Oh, you know the Clover Grove grapevine as well as I do. Someone said Portia didn't approve of the way you managed your cat. Negligent, was the word."

"Negligent! My Fifi is spoiled rotten."

"Portia told people you left Fifi alone overnight, even

entire weekends, and that the stress of abandonment made Fifi pull out her own hair. Portia was planning to report you to Animal Services."

Belle rattled hangers on the rack until a couple of dresses slipped off in a pile of pretty fabric. "Well, I suppose Portia won't have that chance now, will she?"

"No, but other people might. Portia was ornery, no question, but she was known for her kindness and dedication to cats."

"If you're accusing me of something, Ivy, you didn't need to cover for it by bringing your entire family in here to disrespect my designs." She eyed my overalls. "It's obvious that we don't share a vision on style."

I held up a simple pink sheath that resembled the one Drama Llama had ruined for Jilly. "On the contrary. This is something I'd be proud to wear, Belle."

Her expression softened slightly. "Try it on. And then I think you might want to stop by and visit Dina Macintosh at The Hound and the Furry."

"The pet boutique? Why?" I followed her to the back of the store. "I fuel up at the feed store. It's way cheaper."

"Because Dina's husband was having an affair with Portia."

She turned quickly, before I could pull the shutters on my shock.

"An affair?" I said. "Are you sure?"

"Doesn't matter if I'm sure. Dina was sure, and that's what counts."

"That doesn't sound like Portia," I said. "She was committed to cat rescue."

Belle actually laughed. "As if that means anything."

"It seems out of character, that's all."

Opening the curtains to the large, communal changeroom, Belle shoved me inside. "You've been gone too long, Ivy. Affairs are as common in Clover Grove as anywhere else."

Clutching the curtains in the middle, I poked my head out of the top and Keats poked his out of the bottom. His tail was wagging, so I knew he didn't have any major concerns about the designer. "Thank you, Belle," I called as she walked away.

"Thank me by leaving me out of this," she said. "And thank me by not letting your mother get anywhere near my designs again."

"As if I'd even want to," Mom said, standing in front of the mirror in a blue ruffled dress. She did indeed look like a collectible doll. "This frock is a travesty."

"Quiet," I said, as I slipped out of my overalls and into the pink dress. It was a little too tight and a lot too short. In other words, perfect for Jilly.

Poppy sneakily snapped some photos of Mom as she pirouetted in front of the mirror. When Mom saw the phone, she flew at Poppy like an irate hen. Daisy tried to break it up and got clipped in the head for her efforts.

Belle's voice rang out over the fracas. "You rip it, you buy it. Stupid children."

I left the rest of my family in the changeroom and went out to pay for the pink dress. Belle was leaning over a table slicing through fabric with savage precision. Her scissors looked exactly like the gold-handled set I'd seen in Iris's hand while she cut hair.

Not to mention Portia's back the night before.

She set them down with a clatter and came around to ring up the dress. Packing it carefully in tissue, she slipped the dress into a bag and offered a smile that showed her teeth for the first time. I couldn't help noticing that her canines turned in a little, which made her smile seem both sinister and false. With my family's antics, I was sure it was false.

Handing me the bag, she said, "Wear it in good health, Ivy."

CHAPTER THIRTEEN

By afternoon, Jilly had recovered enough to join the next mission. Keats sat on her lap in Buttercup's passenger seat. In the back, a wailing cougar thrashed in a plastic crate.

"That noise is going to bring back my migraine," Jilly said. "Remind me why Percy had to come along?"

"Because Dina's a cat lover, first and foremost. I want Percy to woo her with his feline charms and then we can ask her about her husband's sordid affair."

Jilly rubbed her forehead, wincing. "Feline charms. Seriously. Can we let him out of the crate to shut him up?"

"I'm afraid he'll taunt Keats and we'll end up in the ditch. Imagine how I'd explain that to Kellan."

Now she smiled. "I'm already imagining how you're going to explain to Kellan that you've interrogated three people in less than a day."

"Interrogating makes it sound so official. We're just picking up a nice collar for Percy at the pet boutique. If one thing leads to another, Kellan should be grateful I'm getting some of the grunt work out of the way for him."

"That sounds just like him," she said, laughing. "Grateful for your assistance with his cases."

Reaching behind me, I unlatched the crate door to release the howling cat. "Percy, I'm giving you one chance, and only because of Jilly's headache. If you cause any trouble, this is your final mission." I glanced at Jilly and smiled. "As for Kellan, I suppose grateful is the wrong word."

"Infuriated is the right word," she said, as Percy settled on the back seat and began to groom off the crate cooties.

"As long as he's still infatuated, that's okay. At least, according to Hazel Bingham. This morning she said the secret to holding a man's interest is to keep them off balance."

"That may be true of most men. Even your brother," Jilly said. "I'm not so sure about Kellan." She ran her hand over Keats again and again. If he noticed, it didn't show because his paws were on the dash and his muzzle was to the windshield, helping me drive. "The mysteries of livestock management are probably enough to keep him guessing, right? Being off balance about his police work is too much."

"I'm helping him. *We're* helping him."

"But he wants his girlfriend to be safe. It's bad enough that you're getting trampled by llamas and rolled in swamps by killer pigs."

"I've got a new policy," I said. "If a big revelation comes to me, I'll call Kellan sooner. That's always been my fatal error. Luckily, *near-fatal*. I always put the pieces together a little too late. If I think faster, I can let Kellan do the takedown, instead of Keats."

There was a strident meow from the back seat.

"You mean Keats and Percy," Jilly said. "I believe he had a pivotal role in the last takedown."

"Sorry Percy," I said. "Your scalp-raking maneuver was inspired. But let's all agree to leave the big moves to the armed officers next time."

"Wise decision," Jilly said. Then she sighed. "I suppose a little conversation with Dina wouldn't hurt. She might be more likely to confide in women. Besides, the sooner your mom is vindicated, and the salon reopened, the sooner we can focus on bringing guests to the inn again."

"That's the spirit," I said, negotiating a rather tight parking spot with Buttercup. "And after we get that straightened out, I can take some private driving lessons in the truck. I am fed up with this car's moods."

"You just hate being so conspicuous. It's hard to sneak around in a big yellow jalopy."

"Kellan always seems to know where I've been and it's not fair," I said. "Buttercup is a regular feature on the Clover Grove grapevine."

Jilly stayed where she was as I got out of the car and came around to release the beasts.

"I'm not going to lie, this is embarrassing," she said. "People already talk smack about us and now we're feeding the flames by bringing a cat along for the ride."

"He's even harder to miss than Buttercup," I said, as Percy strutted along the sidewalk beside Keats. Both tails rose like plumes. "Maybe Cori was right about these two being secret buddies. She said they had a joint cause. What could it be?"

Jilly gave me a blatant "duh" look. Her head must still be pounding because she was usually far more subtle. "Their joint cause is protecting you from yourself. You saved them, they save you."

My heart contracted a little at the thought. I didn't want my pets putting themselves at risk for me. That's exactly what Portia had accused me of doing, when it had never been deliberate. It just worked out that way.

"I didn't save Percy," I said, tackling the easier issue. "Edna did that."

"You saved Percy from Edna. He isn't feral and was never meant to live life in the wilds. He's grateful to be sleeping on the pillow beside you and he shows it." She waited a beat before adding, "You'd better wash the pillowcase well if you ever want Kellan to use it."

Now my face ignited. "For someone with a headache, you're awfully chipper."

"Breathing," she said, patting her abdomen. "We need to be on our game here, Ivy."

I paused outside the cute little pet boutique and took two deep breaths. "In for seven, out for seven. This isn't a nine-count situation, as far as I'm concerned. I've met Dina and she's quite nice."

"That was before she was a woman scorned. If the affair comes up, let me take over, okay?"

"Consider it done."

I pushed open the door and a tinkle of tiny bells announced our arrival. Dina Macintosh was on her hands and knees, arranging stuffed dog toys in a basket. Her long, highlighted hair made her look about 40 but I knew she was closer to 50. As hoped, her face lit up when Percy sashayed toward her and she sat down cross-legged to greet him.

"Oh my. I've never seen a more gorgeous marmalade," she said. Percy stepped into her lap, turned twice and collapsed on his back, inviting a tummy tickle. I'd never seen him offer his spotted belly to anyone before.

Keats sat beside me and watched Percy work. Generally, the dog didn't warm to people on first meeting and couldn't fake it, so this seemed like an area where the cat could shine. Percy assumed everyone loved him until told otherwise, and even then he didn't buy it.

"Hi, Dina," I said. "This is my friend Jilly Blackwood, and you've met Keats. The bold gentleman in your lap is Percy. He joined the family recently and needs a new collar and tag. Two in fact, as he conveniently keeps losing them."

"Well, you certainly wouldn't want to lose him. What a fine specimen."

She made no effort to move, so Jilly and I leaned against the counter. There wasn't much room in the small store because it was packed to the ceiling with high-end pet products.

"How's business?" I asked. "Does the change in season affect you?"

She nodded. "There's an uptick as people buy winter coats and boots for the dogs, and warmer beds. That usually rolls right into Christmas, our biggest time of the year." She caught herself and stroked Percy harder. "*My* biggest time. I run the place alone now."

"You mean Roy's found something else?"

"*Someone* else." She eased the cat off her lap and stood up. "I'm sure you heard about Portia."

"That she passed away last night in tragic circumstances? Yes. It was in my mother's salon."

I plucked a rhinestone-encrusted leash off a hook and dangled it in front of Keats. He shuddered as if I'd doused him in water. He was rarely on leash, and this one would embarrass him greatly.

Dina walked over to a rack of cat collars and sorted through them. "It was tragic. But I can't say I'm sorry I'll never have to run into her again. That's the worst part about a breakup in a small town. You can never escape it." She gave a bitter laugh. "Especially when you have a pet store and the other woman is a cat sitter."

I glanced at Jilly and she accepted the baton. "Oh, Dina, that must have been so hard," she said. "I've been where you are, only it was in my workplace. That's like a small town, actually."

With her back still to us, Dina seemed to swipe at her face with one hand. Meanwhile, Percy wove between her legs in a tight figure eight. Each turn featured a stylish swish of the tail that wrapped around her ankle and then unfurled. It was mesmerizing, and her head tilted down to watch.

"Thank you, Percy," she said. "That really helps." Turning with a few collars looped over her hand, she tried to smile but grimaced instead. "It certainly was hard. You know Portia. Imagine what it was like to lose out to someone so abrasive."

"She was that," I said, taking the collars from her and inspecting them.

"I felt the same way," Jilly said. "I couldn't understand why my ex chose a woman so different from me."

"I still don't understand how any of it happened. Portia stayed with our cats from time to time and it was tough following all her rules, let me tell you. At some point when I was staying with my mom in Dorset Hills, I suppose she took up husband sitting, too." She sighed. "I guess I was too nice, because he didn't seem to find her abrasive at all."

"It's not about you," Jilly said. "Don't believe that for one second. If he strayed with Portia, it's a flaw in his character, not yours."

"Thank you." Dina's voice was faint, and she seemed to have diminished before my very eyes. Percy was still working the fluff hard, however, and a few more swishes restored her to normal size. "It's hard not to take it personally."

"Oh, I know," Jilly said. "I beat myself up for a long time, too. But I'm here to tell you that there's life after a cheater. There's love after heartbreak. And there are good men who will treat you right."

Dina stooped and lifted Percy. He lolled in her arms like a ragdoll. "You're very kind, Jilly. And beautiful, too. Asher would be lucky to have you."

"I agree," I said. "She totally outranks my brother."

Dina finally laughed, and we joined in.

"What if Roy comes crawling back now that Portia's... out of the picture?" I asked. "Stranger things have happened."

"I know he had regrets already," Dina said. "But I wouldn't entertain that for one second. Once a cheater, always a cheater."

"You mean they'd already broken up?" I asked.

She shrugged, hugging Percy close. I'd never known a cat to endure that kind of embrace. But his paws flexed and his eyes half-closed. I could hear his purr from two yards away.

"Don't know, don't care," she said. The temperature in the shop seemed to drop sharply. "Roy still has his other love, an ATV. If it tips over and crushes him, well, it would make the divorce simpler. All I want is the store and he's fighting me for it."

She walked around the counter with Percy still in her arms. As she passed, Keats gave her leg a good sniff. His tail was only about half-mast, which said he wasn't overly impressed with Dina. Either that, or he was jealous she was falling all over Percy. There was nothing conclusive, however. It was possible to be unlikeable without being a murderer.

Selecting a couple of the collars she'd handed me, I watched as she rang up the total with her right hand. The left continued to cradle Percy, and as she adjusted the purring load of fluff, I noticed she was still wearing her engagement and wedding rings.

Maybe she was just stringing Roy along to keep the divorce from going through. Or maybe she wanted him back more than she let on. Either way, it seemed at odds with her words.

"Do you think Roy might have had something to do with... what happened?" I asked.

She put the collars in a little paper bag and passed it to me before coming around to surrender the cat. That's when I noticed the gold-handled scissors sitting by the cash register. Someone must have offered a great deal on them because they seemed to be everywhere.

"I would hate to think I was stupid enough to marry a murderer," Dina said. "A cheater is bad enough." She set Percy on his paws and he waltzed over to Keats looking quite taken with himself. "But I sure hope the police find out who did it," she added. "Because I'd like to send them a thank you note."

CHAPTER FOURTEEN

I always hated it when Kellan caught me in the manure pile. I expect most women would feel the same way, and yet it happened to me quite often. When we were getting along well, he tended to drop by unannounced on his lunch hour just to say hello. When things were a little tense, as they were now, he liked to catch me unawares.

Then, too, I spent more time working over the manure than was strictly necessary. Once, I'd fainted from the toxic gas released by stagnant manure and I didn't want that to build up again. Nor did I want any of the dung explosions I'd read about. It would be a terrible way to buy the farm, as it were. Or to lose the farm for that matter.

So that's where I was when Kellan drove in the next afternoon. I caught a glimpse of the police SUV as he rounded the bend, and kept shovelling. There was no point running around the barn and pretending I'd been bathing in rose petals.

Keats left his half-hearted pursuit of Percy in the empty pasture and went to round up Kellan.

Literally.

It would have made me laugh to see this broad-shouldered uniformed man hop like an antsy goat had it not been for the disgruntled look on his face that had nothing to do with the dog.

I was in trouble again. And no wonder, really. It was just a matter of how much he knew about my efforts the day before. I reminded myself to confess to no more than strictly necessary.

"Hey," he said, jerking like a puppet as Keats pulled his strings from behind. "Tell him to stop that nipping right now, Ivy. Do you have any idea what my uniform cuffs look like? There's only one good leg left in the bunch."

I leaned on my shovel and smiled down at him. It was kind of nice to have the height advantage for a change. The manure pile was a good seven feet high and equally wide because Charlie hadn't hauled it off with the tractor for a couple of weeks. "I doubt criminals take that good a look at your cuffs, Chief. If they do, they're probably not guilty. That's how I'd view it."

"You have an interesting way of looking at the law, Ivy. It's a shame we don't always agree."

"Keats, off," I said. "The chief left his sense of humor in the squad car."

"Actually, I lost it at the Bingham manor the night of the murder and haven't found it since."

"Oh? How so?" Turning, I dug deep into the manure. I had a feeling where this was going and it was likely to stink more than the cow flaps.

The dog stood down, but Kellan turned his back to the fence and leaned against it to ward off sneak attacks. Keats liked to wait till the conversation got exciting, which it often did, and then lunge for the win. No matter how many times he did it, Kellan was shocked. I put that down to his being an only child. You couldn't survive a family like mine without learning to keep one eye open for an ambush.

"Let me describe it," he said. "We'd already spent several hours at Bloomers dealing with the situation there. Then I enlisted your brother to come with me to assess the cat situation. Animal Services couldn't take any immediate action, but I wanted to make sure everyone was fed and happy. Because I knew you were worried."

"I sure was," I said, shovelling faster. "Those poor cats, stacked up like mismatched china on the dining room table."

Kellan crossed his boots, settling into the story. "Imagine my astonishment to find not a single cat in the Bingham manor."

"None at all?" Shovelfuls of manure were flying at random now and it was good he'd moved quite far away. "How odd. I saw dozens upon dozens there only a few days ago."

"Not one remained, at least that Asher and I could find, and we covered the house from top to bottom. Your brother even scooted under the beds and behind the furnace for a look-see. It was good of him when the whole place reeked of cat urine."

"So clearly the cats had been there before that. I hadn't imagined it."

"Oh yes. There were litter boxes by the dozen and bowls of food that still looked untouched."

I put my foot on the spade to shove it in deep and expose a new layer. "That's so strange. Do you think Portia had evacuated all of them before... what happened?"

"Possibly. What do you think?"

"If Portia had any idea things were heading south, I

know she would have thought of her cats first. She truly cared about them."

"It would have been heavy work for one woman to catch and move that many cats in just a day or two, no?"

"For sure. But she probably had a contingency plan. Maybe after she saw me snooping she put it in action."

"Ivy." His tone changed and I knew that the uniformed cat was tired of playing with his mouse. "Stop playing with manure and look at me."

I did as he asked. "This work is not a game, Kellan. More farmers die from manure asphyxiation than from lightning strikes every year."

He pushed off the fence and came toward me. "Is that even true? Is a single word you're saying today true?"

Crossing my arms over the spade handle, I grinned. "I don't know if the lightning part is true but it sounded good, right? As for Portia, I fully believe she had a contingency plan."

"More sidestepping of the proverbial cow flap," he said, glaring up at me.

"Is there a proverb about cow flaps?" I asked. "Is that even true?"

He shook his head and smiled at last. "Just tell me what really happened to those cats. You sent the chief of police on a fool's errand in the middle of a murder investigation. I think you owe me an explanation."

Turning, I walked down the steps I'd carved into the manure pile. Jilly called it my stairway to heaven because she knew I found this chore extremely therapeutic. It was true. Whatever crap life flung at me I could work it out on this dung pile, knowing I'd ultimately transform something toxic into fertilizer, out of which beautiful things could grow.

"Do I look like a debutante?" I asked, during the descent. "It might be the closest I'll ever get to a runway."

"You're something else," he said, grinning now. "It's very difficult to stay mad at you."

"Good. Because I don't know what happened to the cats and I would never have knowingly sent the chief on a fool's errand."

He tilted his head skeptically. "I'm sure you have a good idea, being so well connected to the rescue underworld."

I shrugged. "I've heard nothing. Zero. Zilch."

"If we work with the assumption that Portia didn't expect to meet her maker that night, it means that somehow the house got emptied in about three hours. No single person could do that."

"It does sound like a Herculean task." I scuffed at the dirt with one boot to avoid meeting his eyes.

"Give me your phone," he said.

"It's in the barn. I've dropped it in the manure too many times."

"If I went in there to get it, would I find a text telling Cori Hogan about Portia?"

"No, you would not." Now I crossed my arms. "And don't you need a warrant for that?"

"I do not need a warrant to get a straight story out of my girlfriend, no."

I met his eyes at last. "No fair. You can't use the G-word against me."

"A guy's gotta do what he's gotta do if his crap-shovelling woman is doing evasive maneuvers."

Now my heart started jumping around like the baby goats in the next pasture. I was "his woman," which was even better than girlfriend, in my opinion. It was just a matter of time before we extracted "crap-shovelling" from the sentiment.

"Fine. I'll tell you. I didn't text Cori, but Jilly called her on the way home. When you mentioned Animal Services we were worried. These cats don't deserve to end up caged in the pound or euthanized. But I didn't expect Cori's rescue team to take care of it immediately, if that is indeed what happened. They won't tell me anything about it because of you."

"Understandable. Because I could have them all arrested for disturbing a crime scene."

"Mom's salon was the crime scene."

"We don't know exactly what happened where. And we may never know because it probably took at least 10 of them to work that fast. You can be sure plenty of stuff got moved around as they chased down cats."

Sighing, I turned to lean against the fence, too. "I didn't expect that to happen, Kellan. I hoped they'd get the cats out of the pound after they were seized, that's all. I thought Edna deserved a chance to weigh in on homes for her particular cats when she got home." I tried to catch his sleeve as he started pacing. "I wasn't deliberately undermining your authority. It just worked out that way."

He stopped pacing. "And how about your early morning visit to Miss Bingham over at Sunny Acres? Were you in the neighborhood?"

"She's over eighty, Kellan. She deserved to hear the bad news from a friend."

"You two are not friends."

"On the contrary. She's coming for dinner in a few hours."

"You just met her this week and now she's coming for dinner?"

"What can I say, we hit it off. We're kindred spirits." I grinned at him. "You're welcome to join us. Jilly's making something special."

"Thanks, but I've got plenty of work to do solving this murder. There's still a few people to interview that you haven't gotten to first."

"Really? Who?" I tried a disarming smile with a hint of fluttering eyelashes. "I've got some time after I finish this manure management session."

"Like I'd tell you," he said, shaking his head.

"I really don't like your tone, Chief. You might want to sweeten it up a bit."

"Well, you might want to stick to manure management and stay out of my investigation."

"Don't say I didn't warn you."

"Warn me about what?"

The question came too late. An orange missile launched from the dung pile, struck between Kellan's shoulder blades, and bounced off. There was a flurry of black, white and orange paws as the two animals scampered off in the direction of the barn.

I covered my mouth for a moment and then said, "I'm sorry. That was extremely rude. I'll have a word with Percy."

"You do that. And I'll have more words with you later, Ivy."

Kellan turned to walk away with dignity. I wanted to call after him about the four little manure paw prints on his back, but Jilly was always telling me to practice more restraint and now was as good a time as any to start.

CHAPTER FIFTEEN

Miss Bingham was overdressed for the barn in her midnight blue brocade dress but she'd insisted on the grand tour, leaving no pasture unexplored. It was slow going with the walker and the rough terrain, but I admired her tenacity. I hovered behind her constantly, arms at the ready, but with a little extra help here and there, she did very well.

"Dear, it was so kind of you to invite Michael and Caroline at the last moment," she said. "My nephew pops in and out of town on a moment's notice and I never know how to plan. It's not like I can host him at the manor. Normally he takes me for dinner, spends the night at a hotel and then flits off again. They're staying a little longer this time because Michael knows how upset I am about Portia."

"He's retired, I assume?" I asked, letting Keats lead us to his favorite livestock in order. The goats had been first and I knew that the camelids would be last. After Drama Llama's recent stunt, he'd fallen even below Wilma, the aggressive sow, in Keats' pecking order. He could outrun and outmaneuver Wilma. Drama had proven a worthy adversary.

"Michael left a good job at a bank a couple of years back to pursue other business ventures. He wanted freedom to wander a bit with Caroline. They've never had children and seem to enjoy their footloose life."

"I suppose they used to stay with you at the manor?" I asked, easing the walker over the flagstones.

"Actually, no. They're not pet lovers, I'm afraid. Caroline's allergic to cats. Michael finds them sly."

"They are sly," I said, telling her about what Percy had done to Kellan earlier.

Miss Bingham laughed delightedly over the story. "Oh, I wonder who had the nerve to tell the chief about the paw prints down at the station." The fluffy orange cat was frolicking around, chasing leaves and invisible mice. "Percy is quite a character."

Keats fell back to pant up at her, clearly jealous. "It's okay, buddy," I said. "You'll always be my favorite."

He mumbled something back in a disgruntled tone.

"Well, you've been told," Miss Bingham said. "Someone's nose is out of joint."

"Percy's changed the dynamics around here," I said. "Plus I've been running around a fair bit to see what I can find out about Portia."

I filled her in on my discoveries and she clucked in disapproval. "I had no idea about any affair between Portia and Roy Macintosh. Do you think it's even true?"

"Hard to say, yet. But if Dina thinks it's true, that's what counts, I guess."

A gray sedan came down the lane and it struck me that I didn't see many regular cars anymore. Clover Grove was full of pickup trucks, along with some odd cars of character, like Buttercup. This was just a sensible, serviceable sedan that I would have seen by the score in Boston.

The couple that got out was equally sensible looking. I remembered Michael Bingham from the launch party for the salon, where he'd been pleasant to me and attentive to his aunt. He was wearing a nice sports jacket and wool slacks, which you didn't see often in Clover Grove either. There was little left of his gray hair, but he hadn't held onto it desperately, either.

Hazel introduced me again to Michael and then to his wife, Caroline, who had a soft voice and a sweet expression. She, too, was overdressed, in a puff of floral chiffon that screamed Chez Belle.

"Come up to the house," I said, surrendering Hazel's care to Michael and walking ahead with Keats. "My best friend and chef is cooking up a splendid fall feast for us."

Jilly did the honors of showing the guests around the inn. I always considered the inside her domain and the outside mine. It was a beautiful division of labor that exploited our strengths and made us appreciate each other more every day.

After a delicious cider cocktail of Jilly's own creation, we sat down to dinner. Hazel ran her gnarled fingers over the oak surface and pressed her lips together. I knew she was thinking about how her heirloom dining table had been relegated to Portia's cats. Tonight, I would do my best to distract her from what had happened. She deserved a respite.

For once, I felt quite comfortable at the head of the table. Generally I was insecure about my hosting skills, especially as we'd really only had two difficult groups. The Binghams, on the other hand, were all that guests should be. The conversation flowed easily as they asked questions about getting the inn up and running, and then shifted to the "olden days" of Clover Grove.

"Did you grow up here?" I asked Michael.

He shook his head. "My mother, Aunt Hazel's sister, left when she married my dad. But Mom and I visited often from Philadelphia and I always enjoyed it. There was a tree house and a creek where I could fish. Or pretend to fish."

"You were such a good boy," Hazel said, with a fond smile. "Your mother and I could sit on the porch and talk while you entertained yourself till sunset. Cordelia and I were close and the town was so different then. So cultured."

"Cultured?" I said. "In what way?"

"There was a literary society and an art appreciation club. Every year the local theater troupe put on spring and fall shows. We had brass and jazz bands and a marvelous choir." Her eyes glazed with nostalgia. "There was always something going on. A reason to dress up and get out. Now the best we can do is the county fair."

"I had no idea," I said. "Mom never mentioned any of that."

Hazel sighed. "As happens with most small towns, I suppose, the most accomplished people moved on to bigger centers. And eventually, the homesteaders started taking us back to the land. Sometimes I think we've reverted to pioneering days."

I laughed. "Well, maybe we can start a literary society again. Or at least a book club."

"Count me in," Jilly said. "And how about a gastro club? Wine tasting? We could hold events here."

"What a splendid way to revitalize the community," Hazel said. "And bring some business to the inn. You need to spread the word far and wide about this wonderful place."

"We'll post reviews online," Caroline said. "The food is stupendous and the atmosphere so welcoming."

"Thank you," Jilly and I chimed at once.

"We'd love to stay here next time we're in town," Michael said. "It's a shame we didn't know about you sooner, because we've booked a rather dubious motel outside of Dorset Hills. It was all we could find on short notice and we want to be here to support Aunt Hazel."

Jilly and I exchanged glances and reached silent agreement. "You're welcome to stay here if you prefer," Jilly said.

"Really?" Caroline said, her smile giving away how she felt about the "dubious" motel. "That would be so lovely. But it's such short notice and we'd hate to put you out."

I preferred to have time to gear up for guests, but I knew Hazel was struggling over losing Portia, and now the police were picking over her family home. When her eyes lit up, I knew we'd made the right choice.

"Not at all," Jilly said. "I have some new recipes I'm dying to try. You can be my guinea pigs."

"Deal," Michael said. "I know we're in skilled hands."

"Tell me about your old tree house," I asked Michael, as Jilly rose to clear the plates. "I can't imagine Hazel built it."

The old woman gave a hearty laugh, but her smile fled quickly. "That was my brother Aaron. He was a skilled cabinetmaker and fond of Michael." She looked at her nephew and added, "In his own way. Aaron was... well, eccentric."

"He actually avoided me whenever I visited," Michael said. "I don't think he knew how to talk to kids."

"He wasn't much of a talker, period," Hazel said. "These days they call it social anxiety. He was almost a hermit, although he did get out to visit antique shows and estate sales. He was a collector of strange and wonderful things."

"What kind of things?" Jilly asked. "Stamps? Postcards?"

Hazel shook her head. "Figurines, mostly. He had a vast menagerie of handblown glass animals by an Italian artist from New York. I can't recall his name."

"Bertucci?" Michael asked. "Bartolini?"

"Batoli," Hazel said. "That's it. They were pretty but so fragile. I was always afraid to touch them because they became valuable after the artist died. Aaron was such a nature lover. He was always off wandering in the woods, and I think that's why these spoke to him."

"And the stacking things?" Michael said, grinning. "What did those say to Uncle Aaron?"

"What kind of stacking things?" I asked.

"They were like Russian nesting dolls," Hazel said, "only in the shape of animals. The circus animals were his biggest finds. He'd correspond with people in Europe and have them shipped. He'd sell some and buy more."

"What happened to the collection?" Jilly said. "Are they with you at Sunny Acres?"

Hazel arranged and then rearranged her linen napkin in her brocade lap. Keats seemed to sense he was needed and moved from my side to hers. He was unusually subdued tonight, perhaps because Percy was roaming around like a lost soul and wailing from time to time. I'd thought about shutting the cat in a bedroom but then he'd only wail louder.

"I'm afraid I had to sell the collection years ago to keep up the manor," she said. "Some of my investments failed and the place was falling apart. Later, when the market turned, I regretted doing it. Aaron would have been so upset to see his treasures end up in strange hands."

"Aunt Hazel, you had no choice," Michael said. "And honestly, those things were..."

"Michael." She stared at him over her glasses. "Beauty is in the eye of the beholder."

He shrugged. "Well, nesting elephants aren't art in my books."

"I thought they were cute," Caroline said. Her comment surprised me because she'd barely said a word through dinner. In fact, she'd pulled some needlework out of her bag between courses and started stitching and I hadn't noticed till now. She was probably used to Hazel and Michael getting on a roll, but as host, I should have done more to draw her out.

Hazel folded the napkin and set it beside her plate. "I wouldn't want all those eyes watching me from my dresser in Sunny Acres, I must admit. There are plenty of spies as it is."

"I'm sure Aaron would have understood," I said. "He sounded like a good brother."

"Oh, he was. I never felt entirely safe at the manor after he left."

"Left?" Jilly picked up. "Where did he go?"

"That's just it," Hazel said, her eyes filling. "No one knows. One day he was just... gone."

Caroline stuck her needle into the fabric circle and reached across the table to pat Hazel's hand. "Don't upset yourself all over. It was more than thirty years ago."

"To me it was just yesterday." She dabbed at her eyes with the napkin. "I was so sure he'd just taken a jaunt around the country. Every day for a decade I opened the mailbox with hope. But he was truly gone."

"You don't think he..." I let the words trail off.

Michael also reached out to pat his aunt's arm before

picking up the story. "Uncle Aaron's suitcase and some of his clothes were missing."

"And the police never suspected foul play?" I asked, despite a warning glance from Jilly.

"They investigated and eventually closed the case," Michael said, wringing his own napkin. "It's difficult to grieve properly when there are no answers. For years I was angry at Aaron for leaving my mom and Aunt Hazel like that. But I've made my peace with it now. I always wondered if he ended up in Europe, surrounded by art."

"That's what I thought, too," Hazel said. "In my vision, there was a wife."

Michael laughed. "Always the romantic, Auntie."

"Well, why not? I gave the story my own happy ending after enough time had passed."

Jilly skillfully changed the subject after that and kept it out of dangerous channels all through dessert. She was still steering when we saw them out to the driveway, and Michael helped his aunt into the front passenger seat of the car.

Caroline reached out to hug me but stopped when Keats slipped into her path. He knew I wasn't big on that sort of thing with people I didn't know well. In fact, it was a sentiment the dog and I shared.

Jilly covered for me by hugging Caroline herself, and I had to sidestep the dog just to shake Michael's hand.

"He looks after you well," Michael said, as Percy insinuated himself into the goodbye ritual by weaving between feet and yowling plaintively. "You're lucky."

"So lucky," I said, smiling. "But it doesn't take him long to warm up to guests. You'll see that soon enough. We look forward to welcoming you officially tomorrow."

As they drove down the lane, Jilly hugged me, which neither Keats nor I minded at all.

"We're back in business, my friend," she said. "And finally it feels safe, right and good."

"It's about time we caught a break," I said, laughing as the dog and the cat took off in a huge circle in the damp grass. They clearly felt our luck turning, too.

CHAPTER SIXTEEN

I was dreaming about handblown glass figurines dancing in green meadows under a rainbow when something woke me. More specifically, two things woke me. One was staring at me with an eerie blue eye in the square of dim light from the window. The other was sitting on my chest with two paws pressing my windpipe with just a slight hint of 10 claws.

"Percy, are you trying to choke me? And Keats, if he is, why are you just sitting there?"

The cat backed up a little and kneaded my rib cage, purring. He was well satisfied with his efforts to drag me from pleasant dreams at two a.m. By the looks of things, Keats felt the same way. I'd seen that expression before plenty of times.

"Nope. Uh-uh," I told him. "I promised Jilly I wouldn't take any middle-of-the-night joyrides alone and she needs her beauty sleep to be ready for the guests tomorrow."

Keats put his muzzle on the side of the bed and whined.

"I know it seems vitally important in this moment, but it

can wait till daylight. I'm trying to be more sensible, Keats. You should help me, not lead me into temptation."

Now he mumbled something that sounded very persuasive. He was making a good case for whatever it was he thought we needed to be doing at two a.m. What I heard in my head was, *"Have I ever led you wrong before?"*

"I don't know," I said. "It depends on your definition of wrong, I guess. You've led me to some interesting clues, no doubt about that. But sometimes things get a little hairy, wouldn't you agree?"

If the dog had shoulders, they'd shrug. He added a mumble that I took as a taunt.

"Don't you mock me just because I'm showing a little self-restraint. I was a very sensible person before you came along."

I let my head drop back on the pillow and thought about my life before Keats. My stomach roiled a little, and it wasn't just from the rich dinner with the Binghams. There were no green meadows and dancing figurines back in Boston. The days of unrelenting drudgery were broken only by moments of sheer misery as I fired people and destroyed their lives. In the evening, I'd drown my sorrows and loneliness in mindless TV. It was a good thing I hadn't inherited my absentee father's propensity for booze.

Keats waited for me to come to the right decision on my own, but patience wasn't Percy's strong suit. The cat flexed all 10 claws at once and I sat up abruptly. It felt as if I'd been electrocuted. "Hey, that hurt!"

I swung my legs over the side of the bed and dumped the cat to the floor as I stood. He landed with a soft thump and an indignant meow.

"Better than you deserve," I said, pulling my overalls

right over my pajamas and then slipping my arms into a fleece hoodie.

I followed the pair downstairs, with Keats in the lead and Percy close behind. Their tails were up in apparent celebration of their victory. Grabbing a parka, and slipping my feet into boots, I reached for the keys.

"Here's where I draw the line... No golf cart. If you want to go somewhere, we take the safest vehicle. And as much as it pains me to say it, that's Buttercup."

Keats threw me a look of disgust that said, "Wimp."

"We call that compromising, buddy. You want to run off on some mission in the night, but I've made commitments to people who care about me. *Us*, actually."

He resigned himself and trotted ahead of me to Buttercup and waited. For the first time, I noticed Percy weaving around and through Keats' paws. The cat rose on his hind legs to try to head butt the dog under his chin, but Keats was having none of that. He backed away with a low mumble verging on a growl.

"Too much too soon, Percy," I said. "It's always better to wait till you're invited to get that friendly."

Keats mumbled something like, "Never going to happen."

I drove partway down the lane with the lights out. By now I knew each curve like an old friend so it wasn't a huge challenge. Once I was well beyond the house, I flicked on the lights and said, "Where to, boys?"

For some reason, I expected Keats to signal for me to turn right at the highway and head to Edna's house. Instead he put his paw on my lap and stared left.

"Into town?" I asked. "Or the Bingham manor?"

He put his paws on the dashboard to urge me on without answering. Meanwhile, Percy got up behind the rear passenger seat and stared out into the darkness. Watching for tails, I assumed.

"Fine," I said. "You'll let me know when I get there."

The dog grumbled as I slowed at the crossroad leading to the old Bingham manor. The message was clear to keep going.

By the time we entered the town, I had a good idea where we were going, and I didn't like it one bit.

"You're going to get me in trouble," I said. "You're like the bad little brother who starts the mischief and the older kid gets stuck with the blame."

He glanced at me with his blue eye and blinked. The rumble in his throat was something new that sounded like a chuckle.

"Here's the thing," I said. "Some people think the owner is the lead dog. They expect me to make good decisions for both of us." I tipped my head to the back. "And now Percy, too. Instead I'm taking dicey advice from two opinionated animals now."

I passed Bloomers and turned down a side street to park well out of sight.

"You rarely steer me wrong, Keats, so I'm going to take a leap of faith here. The jury's still out on the cat. I can totally see him turning me in if he thinks he can get a better deal."

Percy gave an indignant meow as he slid between the seats and left the car first.

"No offence, Percy. You can't help it. Cats are known for looking out for number one."

He stood on the sidewalk, looking up with eyes that glowed in the darkness. Keats' blue eye was often visible in low light but it didn't reflect as eerily as Percy's.

"Okay, let's make this super fast," I whispered as we hurried toward the salon. "Asher told Jilly the police finished their investigation so at least I'm not disturbing an active crime scene. Bloomers should be cleared to reopen soon."

My key worked in the back door, but I congratulated myself on making the safer choice by entering through the front door. I locked it behind me, keeping my gloves on and phone at the ready. The dog and cat didn't hesitate for a moment, walking swiftly ahead of me to the basement stairs.

"Oh man, I was afraid of this. You want to check out the basement." Percy did a figure eight around my boots. "My heart's going like a jackhammer and you have time for dance moves?"

Keats gave a mumble that normally inspired confidence. Not tonight. Not when there had been a body down there so recently. I didn't want to be next. But I knew well that Keats wouldn't want me to be next, either. His ears and tail were up and his ruff was down. There was no looming threat.

"Fine," I said. "But you'd better come up with something Kellan and his team couldn't find. Use your noses, whiskers and claws, boys."

The animals had tools and talents I never would. Moreover, Keats, at least, had remarkable intuition. He'd probably sensed something the night of the murder and gave Kellan a chance to find it. Now he had to do his officious border collie spot check. He was always the smartest field agent on the case.

Pulling open the basement door, I flipped on my light and held it against my pant leg. "Overhead lights or not, Keats?"

He grumbled a no, as I suspected he would. There were two windows down there that would reveal us to passersby.

That was unlikely, though. After the three pubs closed at one a.m., Main Street was always dead.

"Dead. That is not a good word in this situation." I took the first two steps and then turned to close the door behind me. "But that's all behind Bloomers now. We just need to inspect for clues, right boys?"

My voice sounded nervous and high, but maybe it was just the acoustics of the unfinished basement. It was little more than a brick box with a concrete floor. There were stacked boxes of beauty products in one corner, half a dozen folding chairs no one claimed after the party in another, and cases of bottled water in between.

"Okay, nothing to see here," I said, carefully sidestepping the spot Portia died. "Satisfied?"

At first, Keats and Percy stuck together as they did their survey. They sniffed the boxes first, and Percy leapt on top, probably just because he could. Then he jumped off and landed lightly beside the dog as he moved on to the folding chairs. Keats looked up at me and mumbled an order to move them.

"Yes, sir!" I offered a mock salute and shifted them about a yard along the wall, making a mental note to move them back to the same place so that Kellan would never know I was here.

When the chairs were out of the way, Keats sniffed the brick wall closely. Percy slid under the dog's belly and did the same through Keats' white front paws. This time the dog didn't complain.

I knelt and directed my phone light at the wall, just as Percy reached out and scratched at a brick.

"Huh. That's odd. The mortar's eroded here." I considered taking off my gloves to pry out the brick but remembered the jackknife in the pocket of my overalls. A farmer was rarely without one.

The blade would have done the trick just fine without help from two paws, white and orange, but the boys were enthusiastic. One brick, two, three, four.

I leaned over, aimed my light in behind them and saw a small compartment lined with plywood.

"No way!" I started to reach in and realized my gloves were meant for barn chores, not fine motor skills. Instead, I pulled out two more bricks and snapped several photos of the contents using the flash. "Should I take them? I can't just leave them here. What if someone else gets to them first?"

Neither pet had time to weigh in before we heard a noise overhead. The click of the back door of the salon, perhaps?

Keats, Percy and I all froze, six eyes staring up at the rafters. Just as I started to wonder if I'd imagined the sound, there was the squelch of footsteps. Rubber-soled shoes, I figured.

Never had my gloved fingers worked so fast as I replaced the bricks. My breath came in ragged gasps and the task was all the more difficult with orange paws apparently trying to "help." Finally, Keats grabbed Percy by the scruff and moved him out of the way. The cat went limp instantly, but the moment the dog released him, he sprang to life again. By that time the last brick was in place and I was scrabbling backward over the concrete. Still, Percy pawed at the bricks, as if double-checking my work.

I retreated to the only hiding spot available: under the stairs. Percy dove in ahead of me, and Keats behind. I crawled on my hands and knees until I'd practically folded in on myself under the lowest few stairs. It was the best I could do, but anyone stooping with a strategic beam would see four eyes looking back. Percy had worked his way head-first into a corner that only had room for air. His orange fluffy tail was the last thing I saw before turning out the light. Meanwhile Keats squirmed into my lap and folded himself up, too. Normally his claws would bother me but I found them reassuring under the circumstances.

"What do we do?" I thought. Or maybe I whispered it aloud because Keats pawed my knee gently as if to shush me.

I wrapped my arms around him and pressed my head into his neck as the door creaked open above us. Keats' fur smelled of hay with a hint of manure. Safety. We'd survived worse. We would be okay.

Probably.

Suddenly, there was another click upstairs, and this one ended with a louder sound. A thud? Did the intruder have backup? I lifted my head just a little. There was enough light from the basement door to show dust motes floating in the air.

Then more rapid, squelching footsteps overhead, and the heavier thud of bigger feet. Work boots probably.

The overhead lights came on, and work boots thumped down the stairs. Every thud forced my heart further into my throat.

Before they reached the bottom, someone called, "Ivy?"

At the same moment, Keats lunged out of my lap, gouging my legs and making me scream.

CHAPTER SEVENTEEN

I recognized the voice over my pounding heart at about the same moment I noticed Keats going for the pant cuffs. He grabbed a mouthful and worried it like a puppy with a stuffed toy, complete with mock growling.

"Let go of my uniform you tuxedoed terror, or you'll spend the night in lockup with your owner."

I crawled out on my hands and knees, expecting Kellan to offer me a hand up. Instead he was hopping away and swatting at the dog, trying to serve and protect his uniform.

"Keats, leave it," I said, scrambling to my feet. "We're in enough trouble as it is."

"You most certainly are." Kellan straightened and conked his head on the rafters. I hadn't realized quite how low the ceiling was until that moment. I wondered how many tall cops had bruised heads from the recent investigation.

"What are you doing here?" I asked. "It's three a.m."

He almost straightened again and stopped himself. "Someone called in a suspicious person report and when I heard the description, I decided to come out myself. The caller very specifically said it was a heavyset man in a big yellow car with a black-and-white dog." He stooped and aimed his phone light under the stairs. "And an orange cat."

Percy backed out of the corner, shook himself all over and then began what was likely to be a thorough bath.

"A heavyset man?" I said. "The nerve!"

Kellan actually grinned. "The parka adds bulk. I'm surprised you fit under the stairs."

"Very funny." I glanced up the stairs. "Or maybe your caller meant another tall, heavyset man. There were footsteps just before you came in. Did you see anyone else?"

The smile left his face. "Stay right here. All of you."

Keats ignored that and followed Kellan up the stairs, passing him midway. Percy, on the other hand, continued his personal grooming. It was a common sight but rarely with such intensity.

"We're fine, Percy," I said. "Thanks for your help."

The cat left his paw hanging and blinked at me once before continuing his ablutions.

Kellan clomped back in a moment, with Keats literally on his heels. If the dog weren't careful, he'd get himself kicked and I doubted Kellan would apologize for it.

"The door to the alley was open," he said. "Did you come in that way?"

I shook my head and he pressed his lips together for a moment. "Ivy, do you know how close you came to... *something*?"

"Well, yeah, Kellan. Another minute like that and one of us would have had an accident. And it wouldn't have been Keats or Percy."

Backing away, he sat down hard on the third stair from the bottom. "You can't keep breaking into crime scenes in the middle of the night. If you don't care about your own safety, care about your pets'."

"It was their idea," I said, wishing that sounded a little more... sane.

"Their idea," he repeated. "And which one of them had this brainwave?"

"Probably Keats, but the decision was taken before they woke me. Basically, I'm just the one with prehensile thumbs and car keys."

He put his head in his hands and then shook it slightly. "Honestly. Do you know how that sounds?"

"Of course I know how that sounds. Do you think I wanted to get out of my nice warm bed and crawl around in a cold basement?"

He looked up at me through splayed fingers. "Yes. Yes, I do."

"Well, you're wrong. Do I want to help get to the bottom of Portia's murder? Yes. Do I want my mom's reputation cleared and the salon reopened? Again, yes. But hiding under the stairs in a creepy dark basement is a definite no."

Leaning back, he said, "And what did Keats think he would find here? Or did he say?"

"Not in so many words. I just got the impression that he knew about a clue you might have missed."

He sighed. "We didn't miss any clues. An entire team patted this place down top to bottom."

"I see." I put my hands on my well-padded hips. "So you were just going to leave the treasure for squeaky shoes to collect tonight? Or was that a setup?"

Getting up quickly, he nearly hit his head again. "What treasure? And squeaky who?"

"Squeaky shoes. Rubber soles. He or she was planning

to come downstairs and I can only guess it was to collect the treasure in the hidey-hole. I assume Portia either dropped it off or came looking for it on the night of her demise."

I pointed to the spot on the brick wall where the folding chairs used to be, and then showed him the photos on my phone.

"What is that stuff?" he asked. "Kids' toys?"

"Rare antiques, unless I'm much mistaken. And I believe they once belonged to Aaron Bingham."

"Hazel Bingham's brother? The one who disappeared?"

I nodded. "Tonight she said she'd sold off his collection to keep up the manor. Looks like some are still floating around."

"Show me," he said.

I motioned for Keats and Percy to do the honors since it was their discovery. Keats seemed happy enough to stand back and stare at Kellan while Percy pawed at the location of the loose bricks. I leaned over and used my knife to poke out the first one. My hand trembled and it was harder than ever to maneuver in my gloves. My fingers had cramped around the knife in case I'd needed to use it for much worse.

Kellan pulled latex gloves out of his pocket, put them on and then knelt with his flashlight. As he reached inside, Keats took the opportunity to lick his face.

"Don't, Keats," I said. "Remember how you felt earlier when Percy took liberties?"

There was a merging of grumbles from both Keats and Kellan, but neither sounded terribly disgruntled.

Pulling out the first object, Kellan held it out to me. "Careful."

I used both hands to cradle a glass figurine of a swan. "It's an original handblown Batoli, I think." Placing it on top of the boxes of beauty supplies, I shook a warning finger at Percy. "Be careful."

Meanwhile, Kellan pulled out several more objects, three of which looked like Russian nesting dolls. Two were in the shape of cats and the last a hippopotamus.

"Those are valuable?" Kellan asked. "They look like stuff from a junk store."

"Collectibles. But possibly also stuff you'd see in a junk store. One man's trash..."

"But why are they hidden in the basement of your mom's salon?"

I shrugged. "Maybe Portia stole them or stashed them here for safekeeping. Maybe she wanted to get them back for Hazel because she knew how upsetting it was to part with her brother's art. Hopefully Hazel can enlighten us."

He smirked a little. "Keats can't fill you in?"

"I wish, but his magic only goes so far, it seems. I'm guessing Portia managed to get a key to the place when she used to cat-sit for Robbi Ford."

"Portia didn't have a key the night we found her here, yet there was no sign of forced entry."

"Too bad Mom didn't change the locks when she took possession. It seemed safe enough with Robbi out of the picture but who knows what company she kept?"

Kellan moved the figures off the cardboard box of beauty supplies and then emptied one. There was just enough bubble wrap to give the collectibles a little protection during transport.

"Let's get out of here," he said, at last. "This place is giving even me the creeps."

"You don't have to ask me twice," I said, following him up the stairs.

At the top he turned. "But I do have to ask you twice or

maybe even three times not to run over to Sunny Acres tomorrow to share the big news with Hazel Bingham."

"Can I at least be there when you tell her?" I said. "She'll be thrilled, I know it."

"When you graduate from the police academy, you let me know," he said. "By then I might even be hiring."

"That's unfair! We're the ones who—"

"Ivy, don't push your luck. I admit I'm glad your animals found this stuff, don't get me wrong. But there were other, safer ways to handle the situation."

He let us out of the salon, handed me the box, and locked the door behind us. The police SUV was parked right in front. He put the box in the hatch and then opened the rear passenger door and gestured for Keats and Percy to get in.

Keats didn't wait a beat but Percy had to be encouraged with a gentle nudge from my boot.

"Where are we going?" I asked.

"Back to Buttercup. Then you'll tail me to the farm. Got it?"

"Like no one will notice that," I said, jumping into the front seat before he had a chance to suggest getting in the back with the animals.

"I have no problem being seen with a heavyset man in a sweet yellow ride," he said, making a wide U turn on Main and swinging around the corner a little too fast.

"Careful," I said. "You've got precious cargo."

"Right. Those figurines look like they'd break if you sneezed on them."

"True, but I meant my pets."

He shook his head as he pulled up beside Buttercup. "Follow me closely now. Any diversions and you're all going into the station for a night behind bars. That'll make the basement seem like a palace."

Scowling, I got out and let Percy into Buttercup. Keats, on the other hand, stayed where he was and actually looked away. He was refusing to leave the police car.

"Let him be," Kellan said. "If he wants a ride-along, he can have it."

"But—"

"Ivy," Kellan said. "Do you trust me?"

"Yes." The word blew away on the chill breeze. "With my life, actually."

"But not your dog?"

"Let's just say I don't trust myself—or the world— without him."

He leaned over so he could see me better. "This is his decision. He clearly wants a word with me, man to man."

I sighed. "Fine. Keats, you'd better have a very good reason for this."

Finally the dog looked at me and the eerie blue eye blinked once for yes.

I FOLLOWED the police car closely, but instead of going back to the farm, Kellan turned down the lane to Clover Grove Gardens.

"Why are we here?" I asked, getting out of the car.

Keats jumped out and greeted me with joyful jumping, as if we'd been apart far longer than 10 minutes.

"Keats wanted to come," Kellan said. There was a grin on his face as he joined me.

"It's almost four a.m. and the place is locked. Where's the fun for him here?" I wrapped my fingers around the cold iron fence. "Although we have climbed in and out before. Does Chief Harper do that?"

"He does not," Kellan said. He jingled his key ring. "But he does accept keys to public parks and use them occasionally. Checking for perps, human and otherwise."

"Okay," I said. "But we won't last long in this cold."

"Oh come on. There's enough down in that parka for all of us."

"Percy is taking a pass," I said, as the cat curled up in a ball on the back seat. Keats charged ahead to the gate, always up for a new adventure.

Leaning back into the police car, Kellan pulled out a tall thermos and slipped it under his arm. Then he unlocked the gate, took my gloved hand and led me to our favorite bench.

My disgruntlement faded away as he offered me the first sip of sweet, warm coffee. There was nothing much to be seen in the garden at that hour, so I looked up at the stars instead.

"Can I ask you a question?" Kellan said, after we'd emptied the first cup of coffee and started on the second.

A chill went down my back that wasn't from the late autumn breeze. As with all our interactions these days, it could go either way.

"Sure." I took off my left glove just to feel the warmth of the cup he handed me.

"You said Keats was magic earlier. Do you really believe that?"

Ah. So that's where this was going. He probably wondered if I had a screw or two loose. My stomach clenched and almost pushed the coffee back up the chute. I didn't want Kellan to think I was crazy. But I always had to be true to myself, and to Keats.

The dog jumped up on the bench on the other side of me, and I wrapped my right arm around him.

"If you mean magic as in fairy dust and potions, then no," I said. "But I believe he knows more than a normal dog should. How that works is a mystery to me. He's obviously a high-performer in a brilliant breed. Border collies are bred to observe closely and be endlessly curious. Plus he's got a great nose. I guess that could look like magic when it's beyond our capabilities."

"But sometimes it seems like you're actually communicating with him on another level. I've seen it."

I thought about this carefully before answering. "After my head injury, I feel like I perceive things differently. Sometimes I see or hear things I wouldn't have noticed before and other times it's the reverse. Mostly I think it works to my advantage, but not always."

He sipped the coffee in silence before saying, "Some of my best police work comes from hunches I can't really explain. I assume it's my unconscious mind sorting out all the facts I take in and making connections beyond my awareness. But I don't believe in magic."

"Me either, although sometimes this dog has me questioning what I know about the world." I shivered and Kellan dropped his arm over my shoulder. It was reassuring that he didn't think I was completely nuts. "As for the treasure hunt tonight, it may have looked woo-woo, but I would imagine Keats just used his nose. On the night of the murder, he followed you downstairs, remember? He would have known what Portia touched. What's really amazing about this dog is his memory. I honestly think he wanted to check to see if you'd found it."

There was no need to share that Keats seemed to know that tonight was the time to get to the treasure before squeaky shoes found it. Kellan was already keeping an open mind about something many wouldn't.

Two years ago, I'd have been rolling my eyes over someone claiming to communicate almost telepathically with her dog, so it must be a tough pill for a man of logic to swallow. But there was no question Keats and I had a special connection, even if it was just through the magic of understanding each other's unspoken signals and body language. Maybe we were just hyperaware and more observant than most people and dogs.

What set me apart was my willingness to roll with it. To be open to the discoveries that came my way. I wondered if everyone could have this kind of bond with animals if they let down their defenses. Jilly and Keats now communicated directly quite often, with words and without. My mind no longer put up the barriers and boundaries that once defined me and felt necessary for survival. For that reason, odd as it seemed, I kind of hoped I'd never fully recover. I wouldn't want to give up this connection to Keats for anything. I may not have been able to continue my HR career with the deficits I had, but in my new life, they were at worst minor hindrances and at best major assets.

"That's probably it," Kellan said, sounding as if he was making a case to himself for the unexplainable.

"There's no point overthinking anything," I said. "I mean, except about the case. Have you found anything more to clear my mom?"

He shook his head. "No, but I haven't found anything more specific to tie her to the murder, either. If it helps, I don't think she attacked Portia, even in self-defense. I've known your mother too long." Getting up from the bench, he started pacing. "I just wish she'd stop getting herself embroiled in things without a good alibi. I waste a lot of time proving your mother's innocence."

"I know. I hope you've chatted to Dina Macintosh and Belle Tremblay. They're two of many who had grudges against Portia."

"I'm working my way through the list. Maybe you could leave that to me."

"Of course," I said. "I'm going to be busy with my new guests anyway."

"Glad to hear it." He turned to face me and while I couldn't see his expression, I sensed another warning coming. "Ivy, try not to follow this dog's so-called magic into danger, okay? Keats may be brilliant but he doesn't know everything."

Keats shifted under my arm, as if planning to dispute that, so I squeezed him hard as a signal to desist.

Jilly was right about the value of practicing restraint. Keats could afford to do a little work, too.

CHAPTER EIGHTEEN

T he last time I'd slept past six a.m. was the day before I moved to the farm. But this morning I managed to sleep right through the Aladdin alarm clock, and the rooster kept on crowing until Jilly rapped on my door.

"Up and at it," she called. "We have guests arriving, remember?"

I remembered, and it was nice that the thought brought pleasure rather than the usual dread. Michael and Caroline Bingham were lovely company. This would give us a chance to hit our stride at last.

Keats didn't seem to share my enthusiasm and trailed after me down the stairs. He even let Percy get out the door first, which was a constant point of contention.

"What's wrong, buddy?" I asked, on the way to the barn. "Did you eat some bad crackle yesterday?"

Although Keats had few of the shortcomings of regular dogs, he did enjoy snacking on rabbit and deer scat, of which there was plenty around. Now that mornings were frosty, I could often hear crunching as we walked to the barn. It didn't thrill me, but I reminded myself that dogs needed to be dogs. Especially if they were going to spend the night being superheroes.

"It'll pass," I said. "Although hopefully not while we're driving into town later. Too much of that stuff and you might rot out Buttercup's leather."

He continued to lag as I collected the eggs, and then showed little of his usual verve when he released the livestock. Driving them out of the barn was typically one of the happiest moments of his day. They wanted to run and he loved hitting the "on" switch. It was an explosion of fleece and fur that never got old for me.

By the time we were on the road to town, however, his spark was back and I heaved a sigh of relief. He put white paws on the dashboard and urged me to turn left off Main Street as soon as we entered town.

"No can do," I said. "Jilly made me promise to come straight home with the groceries. Otherwise there will be hungry guests at lunch."

Keats turned his blue eye on me and mumbled something.

"I'm sure it seems important, but it can wait. How about we come back this afternoon once everyone's settled?"

The blue eye continued to pin me, unrelenting.

"Okay, fine," I said, making the next left and circling back. "This errand of yours had better be quick. Jilly deserves to have everything go right this time."

Keats' mouth dropped open in a happy pant that lifted my spirits immediately. Whatever bothered him earlier had passed now. Maybe he was just happy to have an hour of time together without—

"Percy!" The cat emerged from the rear footwell, bounced off the seat and landed on my headrest. "Oh my gosh, you sure know how to make an entrance. But you won't be making an exit this time."

The cat moved over to the headrest on the passenger side, squished against the roof of the car. I knew his strategy. When I opened the car door, he'd slingshot out of here. It was almost impossible to stop him, even with Keats to slow him down.

When I saw the destination the dog had in mind, however, I had a change of heart. His paws bounced off the dash repeatedly to signal for me to park in front of The Langman Legacy, an antique store owned by sisters Heddy and Kaye Langman.

"Okay, got it," I told the dog. "Unfortunately there's a 'no dogs' sign on the door, and if you want me to get information out of them, it would probably be better to ask first."

Seeing his tail and ears droop was a little heartbreaking. And when I released the cat, Keats curled up in a small ball in the passenger seat.

"It's not personal," I said. "These ladies were clients of Portia Parson. They're cat ladies, first and foremost. Establishing that connection really helps with sleuthing."

He tucked his nose under his tail and closed both eyes.

"Buddy, I'll come back for you. I promise."

"Lady, stop talking to your dog and watch your cat," someone said. "I nearly tripped over him."

I turned to find Percy sashaying down the middle of the sidewalk. He'd always had a swagger, but since I'd put a rhinestone collar on him from The Hound and the Furry, he seemed to have delusions of royalty.

Following him to the door of The Langman Legacy, I said, "Can we make this fast, Percy? Keats is upset with me and I really can't handle that."

He looked up at me and blinked once, as if to agree.

Perhaps he wasn't as unreasonable a creature as he often seemed.

I hadn't been in the store since I was a child, but you didn't forget a place like that. Or a smell like that. Not surprisingly, the air was full of... old. Old wood, old leather, old fabric, old books, old wax and old stuff I couldn't even see because the place was so full. I thought I remembered the round oak pedestal table covered in china from when I was a kid, but it probably just looked the same.

The Langman sisters were not antiques themselves, despite having been in business so long. They'd inherited the store from their dad when still in their twenties and were about the same age as my mother. That's the only reason we'd dropped by now and then, because while my mom loved secondhand clothing, that's as far as her interest in "old" went. Her apartment was small and the furniture modern and streamlined.

Kaye was behind the tall oak counter that definitely hadn't changed since my last visit.

"Why, Ivy Galloway, how nice to see you." She got down off the high stool and came around to hug me. I took it like a champ, although I would just as soon have hugged one of my farm animals. Not that there was anything particularly off-putting about her. She looked like pretty much any woman of her vintage in Clover Grove. Hair short and low maintenance. Minimal makeup. Clothes that could take you from grocery store to the neighbor's pot luck and back. I'd probably end up just like that myself, because this apple had fallen pretty far from her mother's tree.

"Nice to see you too, Miss Langman," I said, slipping out of her grasp as soon as it was polite to do so.

"Kaye, please," she said. "You're all grown up now." She

evaluated me as if I were a rare bit of porcelain. "And the prettiest of the Galloway Five, if you don't mind my saying."

"I don't mind, but the other four might," I said, laughing.

"Heddy, come out here," Kaye bellowed. "Ivy Galloway, lady farmer, has paid us a visit."

I managed to slide behind a display table of glass vases before Heddy Langman could snatch me up in a hug, too. "I hope you don't mind but I brought a friend," I said.

"Who?" Heddy asked, peering around. "Where?"

"Percy," I called. "Show yourself."

The cat leapt lightly onto the table I was lurking behind, somehow managing to avoid touching a thing.

The Langman sisters screamed a little louder and longer than the situation really required. Either they had a flair for the dramatic or the vases were more valuable than they looked.

"Ivy, you can't just walk around town with a cat off leash," Kaye said. "People will think you're crazy."

"If he were *on* leash they'd think I was even crazier," I said, shrugging. "Percy stowed away in the car today and I heard you liked cats. I'd like to bring my dog in, too, if you—"

"Nope," Kaye said. "There's a sign on the door for a reason. But we do like cats. I have two and Heddy has three."

Percy wasted no time in beginning his seduction, sinuously coiling around their outstretched arms.

"This is an extraordinary cat," Kaye said. "He's not only handsome, he's also gregarious."

"More social than my dog by far," I said. "And sneaky as heck. I don't even know how he gets past me and into the car but it's becoming a regular thing."

"What does your mom think of him?" Heddy asked, a smirk playing on her lips.

"Oh, you know Mom," I said. "Not much of a pet lover. And now I have over sixty animals, if you count the chickens."

"You've had quite a time of it since you came home from Boston," Kaye said. "That farm's always been cursed, you know."

"Cursed? Really?" I watched Percy rear up on his hind paws to beg someone to pick him up. No takers. "Sometimes I've wondered, I have to admit."

Heddy walked over to a glass jar in a corner. "This is sage. Have you smudged the place?"

"I'm rather surprised to tell you I have. Well, Daisy did right after I moved in. You see where that got us."

Heddy laughed as she snipped the price tag off the sage with familiar gold-handled scissors and then handed the bunch to me. "Smudge again," she said. "But I'm glad you've kept your sense of humor."

"Yeah. I'm the glass-half-full Galloway Girl. If we hadn't smudged once, there could have been even more fatalities."

They both laughed, although Kaye looked slightly scandalized. I'd just provided an excellent sound bite for the rumor mill.

Heddy finally took Percy's bait and picked him up. She let him snuggle into her neck and patted his back firmly as if burping a baby. "What a charmer."

"That's how he gets away with murder," I said. Oops. Poor choice of words. Sound bite number two. I would have to get to business before I set the grapevine completely on fire.

"What can we do for you?" Kaye asked. "Gift for a sister? Or a handsome boyfriend, perhaps?"

"Actually, I was just on my way to get groceries and thought I'd stop in. Mom found some old junk in one of those vintage stores she's always visiting and wondered if it's valuable."

"Probably not," Heddy said, rolling her eyes. "Nothing she's shown us before has been anything special. We make regular rounds throughout hill country so there's nothing we haven't seen."

"That makes sense," I said. "But what if just this one time she found a true treasure?"

"Fine, tell us about it," Heddy said, relenting. It seemed like she couldn't keep up the attitude with Percy wooing her with the purr. "Not another cheap crystal bowl, I hope?"

"A vase," I said, touching one on the table. "Shaped like this one, but a pretty shade of red."

"Cranberry glass," the sisters said in unison.

"Vases like that are a dime a dozen, Ivy," Heddy said. "That won't finance your mom's new venture."

"Figured as much," I said. "A little extra cash would have been nice for her about now."

They nodded in unison, too. "Such a shame about Portia passing where and when she did," Heddy said. "Not that there was any love lost between us."

"Heddy." Kaye eyed her sister. "We were on good terms with Portia for many years. She minded our cats and even the store when we travelled. Few small business owners have the luxury of vacations."

"But then she went nuts," Heddy said.

"Heddy!" This time Kaye sounded like the older sister she was. "Portia was clearly cracking under strain. She wanted that manor so badly but had no idea how much it would cost to maintain. I offered to help her out by buying some of Hazel's old things but she wouldn't hear of it."

"Personally, I got tired of Portia's lectures," Heddy said. "Mostly she ranted about brushing my cats regularly. Then last spring I came home from a trip to find she'd shaved three of our five. For their own comfort, she said. They looked ridiculous."

Percy pulled away to stare at her with wide eyes.

"It's almost as if he understood," Kaye said, reaching out to pat him. "It's okay, handsome. We fired her after that. And then she badmouthed us as terrible pet owners."

"Which didn't help our reputation in this homesteading town," Heddy picked up. "Clover Grove isn't far behind Dorset Hills with its fads."

"We had no choice but to cut her off completely," Kaye continued. "And since we have so many friends in town, her work dried up quite a bit, I'm afraid."

"I'm really not surprised someone stabbed her," Heddy said.

"Heddy!" This time Kaye was so exasperated, she took Percy out of her sister's arms and handed him to me.

"Well, it's true," Heddy insisted. "I'm only surprised it was Dahlia. I didn't think she had it in her."

"*Heddy!*" Now the protest came from me. "You're friends with my mom and you know full well she couldn't murder anyone."

"I suppose not," she said, grudgingly. "Even if she wanted to, Dahlia's always been a delicate flower. There may be another explanation."

"I'm quite sure the police will find out what it is," I said, setting Percy on the floor. "Then Mom will get to reopen, instead of spending her time in junk stores. This week she came home with these crazy stacking dolls. Only shaped like a rhino."

The glance they exchanged was so fleeting I might have missed it if I weren't watching closely.

"A rhinoceros? How odd! Are you sure?"

"Well, it may have been a hippo. Or a manatee. Something fat, I think. What I do know is that there were five of them, each smaller than the last, and they fit together like a dream."

"It sounds like a child's toy," Heddy said. "I doubt it's worth a dollar, but we'll take a look at it, if you like."

"Okay, I'll bring it along next time I'm in town."

"Or we could visit and save you the trip," Kaye said. "You must be so busy handling all that livestock."

Handling livestock, especially Wilma, the bottomless pit, had shown me what true hunger looked like. Kaye and Heddy were starving for the nesting hippo doll recovered from the salon hidey-hole, that much was clear. There was a gleam in their eyes I'd seen on other collectors. Their craving would never be satisfied because there was always something more to acquire.

"No hurry. Mom isn't sure she'd want to sell anyway. She might save it for her next grandkid—if she ever has one. Daisy's done and the rest of us are in no hurry."

"Now we're curious," Kaye said. "And after nearly forty years in the business, there isn't much in the way of collectibles we haven't seen."

"I can believe that," I said, turning to head for the door. A spot of orange made me look up to find Percy sitting on a tall shelf beside a glass case. He turned his sharp green eyes to look inside, and I saw a glass figurine of a bear that looked very much like the original Bartoli creations Kellan had taken into custody. Right beside it sat a wooden circus poodle. Unless I was much mistaken, it was the smallest in a set of stacking dolls. Perhaps they kept the rest out of sight.

"Where's the cat gone?" Heddy said.

By the time she finished her question, he was weaving through her feet.

"Will you come out to the car and meet my dog?" I asked. "He's in a terrible funk that he couldn't come in."

"Anything for Dahlia's girls," Kaye said. "Say hello to her for us, will you? We've wanted to reach out but figured it was better to let the dust settle first."

"She understands completely. Everyone who had words with Portia is a little on edge right now. But we'll all get through this together as a town, right? That's what Clover Grove does."

When we got to the car, the women oohed and aahed over Buttercup, a collectible that was apparently well worth having. Keats unfurled from the passenger seat and got out to say hello.

The Langman sisters weren't dog lovers, and seeing his ears flatten and his hackles prickle did nothing to change their opinion.

"I'm sorry," I said, letting both animals into Buttercup and sliding behind the wheel. "He's been a little moody since Percy arrived to steal his thunder."

"If you ever want to give that cat up, I know the perfect home for him," Heddy called, as the car's engine turned over and let out quite a roar. "Mine."

"At least I know he'd never be shaved," I said, waving merrily as I pulled out into traffic.

CHAPTER NINETEEN

Jilly was gifted in many things, headhunting and cookery chief among them. Spontaneous event planning turned out to be another. When I told her I wanted to hold a celebration of life for Portia, she was on board before the words were out of my mouth.

"I don't even care what you're scheming," she said, "and I know you're scheming something. What I see is an opportunity to gain back some credibility for both the inn and the salon, and do something nice for the Binghams at the same time. Let's do a fundraiser for cat rescue while we're at it."

"Perfect. It's a win all around," I said. "I feel bad there's no one to arrange a funeral for Portia. It seemed that she had few friends left, other than Hazel Bingham."

"That is sad," Jilly said. "And commendable of you." She grinned at me as she reached for a notepad to start her first list. "Plus it might bring together quite a few suspects in Portia's death. I'm sure you'll fire off some probing questions as you show people around."

"You know me so well," I said, grinning back. "Should we run into town and set things up?"

She grabbed her purse and coat. "If we're doing it on Saturday, there's not a moment to lose."

Nonetheless we lost half an hour locating Percy and containing him in the laundry room, which now had a bed, litter box, food and water. He was hardly suffering, but you wouldn't know it from the caterwauling.

"Why do I feel so guilty?" Jilly asked, getting into Buttercup's passenger seat. Keats climbed into her lap without waiting for an invitation. Now it was just understood and she kept a towel on the floor to protect herself from his claws. The ride was generally smoother in Buttercup than the truck but without power brakes and steering, it was no magic carpet.

"Percy's wheedling his way into our hearts," I said. "And he's proving to be useful, too. But cats aren't welcome in nearly as many places as dogs and we have a lot of stops today."

"I worry about him when he's with us," Jilly said. "For such a noticeable cat, he's a master of evading notice. He could so easily be lost."

"Percy has his own agenda. At the same time, I admire his independent spirit."

The dog turned to give me a baleful look.

"Time to suck up," Jilly said.

"Keats, buddy, I like the cat but I *adore* you."

He swished his tail in Jilly's face to acknowledge my effort.

"So where are we really going?" Jilly asked. "I feel a mission beneath the errands."

"Again, you know me so well. I just thought with our guests off admiring the last of the fall leaves, you might throw a little charm at another suspect. Hazel put me on to this one, too."

"Just how many people did Portia offend?"

I shook my head and sighed. "She'd gone from being everyone's favorite cat sitter to being pretty much jobless. That must be why she had to hit up Hazel for cash all the time."

"It's so strange. Something devastating must have happened to cause that change."

"Well, a bad breakup can do that, right? If that's what happened with Roy." I thought about how long I grieved for Kellan after our college breakup. I'd been the one who'd pulled the trigger, but only because I felt so unfairly treated. He'd been told—and believed—I was cheating on him and both of us were too proud to talk it through. All those years wasted...

I must have sighed, because Keats rested his muzzle on my lap and Jilly patted my arm.

"It's all good now, my friend," she said. "Leave the past in the past."

"You're right," I said, sighing deliberately this time. "The more I learn, the more I want to find out what happened with Portia. How did Aaron's collectibles come to be in her possession? What did she plan to do with them?"

"The truth will come out in the Clover Grove wash. It always does," Jilly said. "Now, who are we meeting behind Kellan's back today?"

"This is where I mention yet again that you're the best friend in the world, right?"

"It certainly bears repeating," she said. "Honestly, I can't hear it often enough."

We pulled up as close as we could to Grassroots Organic Meats and got out of the car. "Keats, I hate to tell you this, but dogs aren't allowed here, either." Once again, he curled up in the passenger seat with a huff of disapproval. "I'm worried about him," I told Jilly as we walked to the store. "He's been a little down lately."

"When's the last time you two walked in the meadows... alone?"

I tried to think back. "Not that long. Maybe a week or so?"

"If you have to think that hard, it's been too long. You're busy, but you both need that time to regroup." She fluffed her hair and pinched her cheeks. "I'm sending you out this afternoon, whether you like it or not. There's no need to worry about Michael and Caroline. If only all guests could be this easy."

"Such a relief, isn't it? This is what innkeeping should be."

"And with just the two of them, I can make spontaneous decisions about meals. If I see something here that looks good, I may even grill. There aren't many good days left."

I pushed open the door and we went into the butcher shop.

"Hi there," Jilly said, directing her best smile at the burly, bald man behind the counter. "What do you recommend for late season grilling?"

"Can't go wrong with a grass-fed steak," he said, eyeing her appreciatively. "But ribs are always a crowd-pleaser and they're on sale."

"Let me think for a minute," Jilly said. "These are big decisions when you run an inn. It can be steak it or break it."

I laughed. The bald man didn't. Strike one.

"Do you have any knuckle bones?" I asked. "I'm trying to bribe my dog to like me again."

"Lady, if you have to bribe your dog to like you, you've got a problem," he said. "Not that I'm big on dogs."

Strike two for not liking dogs. Strike three for calling me "lady."

"Everyone likes dogs, Silvio," I said, after straining to see his name tag. "Isn't that almost a prerequisite for surviving in this town?"

"I moved here from Dorset Hills to get away from that crap," he said. "My cat couldn't even go outside there anymore. The mayor wanted to ban them completely."

"I heard about that," I said. "But there's a new mayor now."

"Too little too late. Their loss is Clover Grove's gain." Now Silvio smiled, showing several gold crowns. He also had a couple of sleeves of tattoos under his white T-shirt and white apron.

"If you're a cat lover, you must have known Portia Parson," I said.

More gold flashed. "Portia? Yeah. Shame about what happened. She used to stay with Buster when I was away, but then she overstepped."

"Oh?" I pretended to eye a whole chicken but the sight of little quills made my stomach queasy. It was hard to disassociate this "meat" from my generous hens. "What happened?"

"She thought she could tell me how to treat my own cat, that's what happened. Buster shouldn't be outside, because he'd get hit by a car. He shouldn't hunt mice because he'd get poisoned. He shouldn't climb up on the cupboards because he'd fall. In other words, Buster shouldn't be a cat, but a decoration."

"Ah. I heard she came on pretty strong. She shaved Heddy Langman's cats because they were too hot."

He pressed his lips together, which I actually preferred because the gold teeth were unnerving me. "See what I mean? Arrogant. But I put up with her until she stuck her nose into my love life."

"That is overstepping," I said.

"Right? I was seeing this new girl and Portia didn't like me leaving Buster alone. Although that's exactly what I was paying her for—to make sure he wasn't alone. She said I needed to get a second cat to give Buster company. But this new girl, she had allergies. One cat was bad enough. So then Portia offered to take Buster off my hands and I said no. You never know how it's going to work out with a girl but I loved that cat. He was a real character."

"*Was?* What happened?"

He started rearranging steaks on a display tray behind the glass with gloved hands, and I had to look away. It reminded me too much of Heidi, Clara and Archie, my cows.

"So, I hired Portia for the weekend and went to visit the girl," he said. "When I got back, Buster had gone missing. She hadn't even called me. Her story was that she was too busy searching. She'd put posters up all over the neighborhood to make it look legit."

"But you thought she'd taken him?"

"Oh yeah. I drove out to the old Bingham mansion to get him back. I looked in the window and saw tons of cats. Not Buster, but enough to call Animal Services on her. I told her to give me back my cat and we'd leave it at that. But she wouldn't do it. Instead she called the cops on me. Threatened me with a restraining order. You can't have that kind of trouble and run a business." He stopped turning the steaks and then rubbed his gloved hands on his white apron. "Man, I wanted to kill her."

His eyes glazed over for a second and then cleared. "I couldn't though. I mean, I could, obviously." He gestured to the knives on the long counter behind him. "But not until I got Buster back."

"And that didn't happen?"

He shook his head. "Someone got to her first." Wiping his hands on his apron, again, he left a long bloody streak. "I went back to the old house the day after that, thinking I could find Buster, but all the cats were gone. Dozens of them. I tried Animal Services but he hasn't turned up."

"I'm sorry to hear all this," I said. "I hope you get him back. But at least it worked out with the girl."

He shook his head. "I can't do allergies." He looked down the counter at Jilly, who was still examining cuts of meat with intense interest. "Your friend like cats?"

"Dog lover first and foremost. Walk us out and you can meet the lucky fella."

Jilly settled on the steaks, which I would not be eating, and kept up a brave smile as Silvio shone some gold while wrapping them in brown paper and tying them with string. I wasn't even surprised when he used gold-handled scissors to snip the string. A local store sold a lot of them.

Then he carried our bag outside and slapped Buttercup's trunk as if she were a prize filly.

Keats got himself back on the job and sniffed the butcher with far more enthusiasm than I felt.

"Not guilty," I told Jilly as I got in the car. "At least, innocent in the court of Keats. But I can't help thinking Silvio bought off the judge with those knuckle bones."

CHAPTER TWENTY

I had seriously underestimated the appeal of our celebration of life gathering for Portia Parson. Cars poured down the lane long before the event officially started at noon. I knew full well that about half attended out of sheer nosiness—to see the farm, to see how the Galloways were holding up under the barrage of bad luck, and to see if anything dramatic might unfold.

The other half came for the free food. Jilly and Mandy McCain hadn't prepared nearly enough, so we sent Asher and Poppy into town to scavenge what they could from the Berry Good Café and other local eateries.

"What a turnout," I said to Hazel Bingham as Keats and I escorted her to see the goats. The crazy dancing kids were her favorites and I wanted to get her there before the throngs got too dense. She had only brought her cane and had to be extra cautious. "We should have made it pot luck."

She looked around and shook her head. "They should be ashamed of themselves. None of these people liked Portia and it's disrespectful to pretend otherwise."

"Probably true about the majority," I said, relieved to

deliver her safely to the goat pasture, where she could grip the fence for support. "You know Clover Grove loves any excuse to gather and collect fodder for the gossip mill. This farm has always been a good provider of compost for that cause. Still, I think a few people genuinely liked Portia, or at least they did until she started going off the rails."

"I still don't understand it," Hazel said, sighing as she handed me her cane and folded her arms on the fence. She was wearing a classy black wool coat over an equally classy black dress, and her hair was coiled in a silvery twist. "What happened to make Portia so stressed and why didn't she tell me about it?"

"I can't help but think it had something to do with your brother's collectibles," I said. Kellan had already informed Hazel about their recovery, although she wasn't permitted to see or reclaim them while they were evidence. "Her prints were all over them. Do you know how they came into her possession?"

"No idea. Those were some of Aaron's favorite pieces. I sold them last, and only when I felt I had no choice. That was about fifteen years ago, when the manor flooded and needed major repair work. I'm sure I told Portia about it at the time. Maybe she found them and bought them back for me."

"Wouldn't she have told you, knowing it would bring you such happiness?"

She shrugged. "I would think so, especially after my health scare last year. Who knows how long I'll be around? But I feel like I don't know anything I thought I knew anymore. It's disheartening."

Tears pooled in her eyes and I quickly pointed to the goats. "Check out the little brown one with the blue eyes. Our newest addition. I'm going to let you name him."

That diversion worked perfectly, and she was still working on goat puns when I delivered her safely to the porch swing and beckoned Teri Mason, artist and friend, to join her. I wanted Hazel to have a shield from the masses, given that I had to circulate and guard the flock. Teri was happy to oblige. Hazel would have preferred Keats to keep her company but I needed him even more than she did in that crowd. Moreover, Keats was unusually anxious himself. Normally he loved a crowd but today his tail and ears told me he wanted custody of his farm back.

When I stopped at the food station—long tables with harvest-themed salads, casseroles and desserts—Jilly took the opportunity to run inside.

I grabbed the last pumpkin pie square, smirked at Mandy, and then bit off a good chunk. "So much for being a good hostess," I mumbled around it. "Most of these people don't deserve your fine work."

Mandy laughed. We were quickly healing the rift that opened when Lloyd Boyce had been murdered. I understood why Mandy hadn't been forthright about her situation with Lloyd and I'd always liked her back in our school days. Time was taking the edge off. No one was perfect, including me.

"I agree with you," Mandy said. She would never have said something like that before but she was becoming more assertive now that she ran Mandy's Country Store on her own. Since she'd been painfully shy all of her life, it was nice to see her evolution. "I wonder how many of them contributed to Portia's anxiety during her last months. She lost most of her business and started falling apart. At the end I was running a tab for pet supplies I knew she would probably never pay, but I didn't mind. I know what it's like to feel like an outcast in this town."

"Did she confide in you about what was going on?" I asked, licking my fingers with the last bite. It was good to know that while anxious myself, I could still enjoy a delicious treat. I reached over to take the last sugar cookie and gave it to Keats. His tail rose and fanned with the rare snack. "I saw her at your counter often."

"Mostly we talked about cats," Mandy said. "That was her comfort zone. I knew from the volume of food she ordered that her numbers were going up and up. I assumed she was worried about Animal Services giving her trouble." She pulled a fresh box of pumpkin squares out of a cooler under the table and I took one of those, too. "Portia thought they were already onto her. She said intruders had been on the property and even broken a basement window. But she wouldn't report it to the police in case her cats were seized."

"Her hands were tied there," I said, washing down the square with the paper cup of coffee Mandy handed me.

"Exactly. So she wasn't sleeping well, always afraid someone would break in. I suggested she at least get a security camera, and offered to order it on her tab."

"That was kind of you, Mandy. Did she take you up on it?"

She shook her head. "And if she ordered anything herself it didn't come through the store's post office."

"Are you going to leave any of those for me?" Michael joked as he joined us with Caroline. They were both dressed down in country casual but still had the city shine on them. That didn't seem to wear off until you'd been rolled in the muck enough times to blend.

Mandy quickly served him a square on a paper plate and said, "I know these are a favorite of Ivy's, so I put a box in the fridge inside."

"Well, I hope Heddy and Kaye don't find them first," he said. "They were taking a tour of the inn."

"Taking a tour?" I said, snapping to bring Keats back to my side. He had formed a canine barrier between me and the crowd and I'd trip on him if I wasn't careful. I was never careful enough. "On their own or with Jilly?"

"Jilly's over there," Caroline said, pointing to my best friend, who was circulating with apple cider on a tray.

"Excuse me," I said. "I'll just make sure Heddy and Kaye get the royal treatment. Thanks for the heads-up, Michael. Now go and enjoy yourselves."

"We already are," Caroline called after me. "It's wonderful to see the community come together like this for Portia. I underestimated Clover Grove."

"Me too," I said, running up the stairs. I had a very good idea why the antiques dealers were roaming around inside the inn, and while they wouldn't find what they were looking for, I didn't want them casing the place out. Asher still wasn't back from town and Kellan had been called away almost as soon as he arrived. That was the downside of dating the chief of police. Luckily the upsides were many.

The sisters were in the family room when I joined them. Kaye was holding the tray that normally sat on the old oak chest that served as our coffee table. Meanwhile, Heddy had opened the chest to look inside.

"Ladies," I said. "Can I help you find something?"

Kaye jumped and the array of tea candle holders clattered on the tray. Heddy dropped the lid of the trunk with a bang.

"We were just looking for that gorgeous cat," Heddy said. Despite the guilty slam, her smile was audacious. "Percy, right?"

"I never lock him in the trunk," I said, with a laugh that

sounded false even to me. "I think Animal Services might frown on that."

"Oh, I know," Heddy said. "What I meant was that we were looking for him and then I saw this trunk. No antiques dealer could pass this beauty by. It's in very good condition. What would you want for it, Ivy?"

"Not interested in selling at the moment, thanks," I said, letting Keats circle and herd them out. His tail was down and his ruff at half mast. He didn't like the sisters at all. "Hannah Pemberton left it behind so it has sentimental value."

"Ah, sentiment," Kaye said, appearing not to notice being subtly pressed to the door. "We can't afford to get attached to things in our line of work."

"Easy come, easy go," Heddy chimed in. By now they were in the front hall and she looked a little surprised when the door opened and Jilly came back in. "Since we're here, we'd love to see the items you came into the store to tell us about."

"They're not here," I said. "In fact, I believe Mom already sold them." Turning to Jilly, I said, "Where's Asher? Can you tell him I need him to help me reach something in the kitchen?"

She texted promptly but it was unnecessary because hearing his name had the desired effect of ridding the house of pests.

As the sisters went down the front stairs, I called after them, "I think the cranberry glass vase might still be available if you're interested."

Heddy raised her hand and I could have sworn there was a little Cori Hudson finger flare in the gesture. But maybe I was wrong. It was turning into that kind of day.

"I'll get Daisy in here to watch the place and then go

and warn Mom about the Langman vultures. She knows about the setup but I didn't think they'd take it this far."

"The Langmans would be hard-pressed to get through the crowd around your mom," Jilly said, grinning. "She's drumming up plenty of barbershop business for when they reopen."

I groaned. "Oh great. She's got a legit way to add constantly to her rotation now."

"Don't worry about Dahlia," Jilly said. "Worry about Roy Macintosh. I happened to be serving Dina lemonade when he pulled in. She dropped a few choice words and then left in a hurry."

"Interesting," I said, looking down. "Shall we go have a chat with Roy, Keats?"

He mumbled agreement but it didn't sound very enthusiastic.

"What's wrong with him?" Jilly asked.

"Not sure," I said. "He hasn't been quite himself lately. Senna York will probably show up today and I'll get her to give him the once-over. As far as I know, she liked Portia and someone had to be providing vet services off the record. I'd vote Senna as most likely to thumb her nose at the County."

"Be careful," Jilly called after us, as we ran down the front stairs.

Her warning was unnecessary. Roy Macintosh was far from threatening, at least in appearance. In fact, he made an unlikely Lothario. He was paunchy, balding and had a pronounced overbite. Or perhaps it was a receding chin. Either way, he didn't initially seem like a hot enough ticket to have two women fighting over him. Mom always said there was a lid for every pot, and this lucky pot had two.

I'd shopped in The Hound and the Furry often enough

that I didn't have to introduce myself when I joined him beside the pasture containing the llamas, donkeys and Alvina the alpaca.

"Hey, Ivy," he said. "I heard your alpaca dances. Where do you hit go?"

"Oh, she's fickle," I said. "She needs to be in the mood."

His smile was kinder than I remembered and his blue eyes crinkled in the corners. Now I was seeing more of the attraction.

"Ah," he said, with a wink. I knew he wanted to add, "Like all women," but was wise enough to hold it back. "I hoped she would. I think Portia would have liked that for her celebration of life."

"Maybe. To be honest, Roy, she didn't think much of me or my livestock handling, though."

He leaned against the fence and sighed. "She wasn't herself toward the end, Ivy. Don't take it personally."

"It was hard not to, when she threatened to start a petition against my farm. But I heard she was under a lot of stress. Perhaps you would know better."

He rubbed one hand over his balding head rather roughly. Too much of that and he'd lose the rest of his hair.

"I guess you've heard what happened between us," he said. "But it wasn't as bad as you probably think."

"I don't think anything in particular. There are two sides to every story. Who would know that better than me?"

"Dina and I had split," he blurted. "She threw me out and I didn't learn till later that she was seeing Al Geeter, the guy who runs the motorhome dealership. No one talks about that whereas I got the bum rap for starting to date Portia."

"Ah. Well, that seems unfair. Were you at least happy with Portia?"

He nodded. "At first, yeah. She was passionate about her work. A good person." He glanced at me. "I thought so, anyway. But over the months she changed. She got moody. Jumpy. Suddenly she was collecting more and more cats at the manor. I didn't want to go over there anymore because it stank of pee. And she didn't want to leave, even for a few hours. She was more worried about those cats than about me."

"Everyone says they saw a huge change in her, Roy. Any idea what caused it?"

He shook his head. "It was subtle at first but turned into complete paranoia. Finally she just snapped and said, 'I can't do this. Not with them after me.'"

"*Them?* Who was them?"

"As far as I know there was no one 'after her.' I mean, she was starting to annoy people but I don't think anyone would take it that far."

I thought about Silvio the butcher going out to Portia's and threatening her. "Some might, Roy. Someone did, I guess. People feel strongly about their pets, and Portia may have rescued some that already had good homes."

"She couldn't stop herself, and I didn't know how to help." His eyes filled. "I hoped it could work out between us later, when things settled down for her. But the last time I went over she just stared at me through a crack in the door. All I saw was crazy-eye, you know? And the cats were trying to get out. She asked to borrow my ATV a couple of weeks later and I dropped it off. Not so much as a thanks." He looked back at Alvina. "And then she was gone."

"Will you and Dina patch things up now?" I asked.

He turned toward me quickly and his blue eyes were cold. "Never. She's trying to take the store from me. And my ATV. Even the cats. She'd leave me with nothing and I wasn't the one who cheated."

Glancing down at Keats, I saw that while the dog was still unsettled, he hadn't reacted strongly to Roy. So I snapped my fingers in the pen to get Alvina's attention. She came over quickly and I told Roy to stand back.

"She spits," I said. "Usually you'll see that crazy eye you mentioned before it happens. But if you jumped around out here, I bet she'd dance for you."

"I can't just jump around," he said. "There are too many people watching."

"Who cares?" I said. "If there's one thing I've learned since I came home it's that you have to dance like no one's watching. So dance hard, Roy, and see what happens."

Finally he gave me a little smile, and flapped his arms. I gestured for him to hop and he did. That was enough to galvanize Alvina. On the other side of the fence, she gave a hop, too. And when Roy started skipping along the fence, she bucked her heels in joy and took off after him.

His laughter caught fire in the crowd and whatever Portia may have thought about the event, I knew Roy, at least, celebrated her life with gusto that day.

CHAPTER TWENTY-ONE

Mom may not always have been present in body or spirit as we were growing up, but I had to acknowledge she'd managed to instil certain principles and values in all of us. Or perhaps she just instilled them in Daisy, who did the heavy lifting with the remaining five. Either way, it started with Mom because our father—I refused to call him dad—had no principles whatsoever. To my knowledge, not a single dollar had flowed to Mom to raise six kids after he left. And to my knowledge, none of us had ever heard from him again. I had to caveat that because there was plenty I didn't know about my mom or my siblings, and not just because I'd stayed away so long. After all, one of Mom's principles was keeping a certain measure of privacy about our individual and family dealings. Despite our frequent too-much-information family meetings, all of us had a few secrets. Except Asher, perhaps. The golden boy was an open book.

One thing we all learned young was our family "safe word." We could call anytime, day or night, say the safe word, and anyone who could come *would* come to our aid.

It wasn't unlike the Rescue Mafia's 911 notification. Only with Cori at the helm, their safe word would never be "butter tart." That was technically two words, but they were enough to send a chill down my spine. Before I left for college, we'd rescued Daisy from home invasion, Asher from two back alley ambushes long before he was a cop, and Poppy from many an unsavoury situation she could have avoided.

When I was putting the livestock to bed after the celebration finally ended, Mom called me and said, "Darling, could you swing by the salon with some of Jilly's classic butter tarts? The Langmans have dropped by for tea and I have nothing to serve them." She gave a tinkling laugh. "Such a faux pas!"

"Be right there," I said.

I dropped the pitchfork and ran, leaving the cows hungry. Keats was on my heels, his blue eye glowing up at me. I called Jilly and told her to meet me at the car. Then I texted Kellan and the rest of my siblings while I waited. Mom hadn't used the code when Portia died, either because she was in shock, or because she didn't want the rest of the family to know until necessary. This time she obviously didn't feel quite as alarmed. But still, those Langmans weren't to be trusted.

Jilly jumped into the passenger seat, dressed in pajamas and rubber boots, and panting. She was holding a tin Mandy had left behind and whatever was in it had no doubt crumbled during the run. It wasn't butter tarts, I knew, but it was only a prop anyway.

The old yellow car took that moment to pass out. "Come on, come on," I said, turning the key in the ignition again. She was unresponsive. Dead.

"Let's go," Jilly said, jumping out. "We'll need to take the truck."

Now I was doubly worried. The antiques oddballs had my mom cornered in the salon and I had to make peace with my automotive enemy to get there.

This time I caught an orange flash from the corner of my eye as Percy slipped into the back seat with Keats. Well, there was no time to evict him now. If he was that desperate for an adventure, he was about to get it.

Jilly braced herself on the dashboard with her right hand and called Mom with the phone in her left. I was astounded that she could carry on a cheery conversation about the finer points of pastry and filling while lurching through my perilous shifts and one seismic stall at a four-way stop. The dog and the cat had retreated to the rear footwell, which Keats only did when the conditions were particularly bad.

Nonetheless, we reached the salon before anyone else, including two of my sisters who lived right downtown. I pulled up on the sidewalk and gave the truck a grateful pat before leading the others into the salon.

"Darling," Mom trilled, as the bell jingled overhead. "You're just in time for tea. The police left the place in a state so I had trouble finding the orange pekoe. Heddy, Kaye and I agree it's the only tea worth drinking. And would you believe they've never had a butter tart?"

"Well, you ladies are in for a treat," I said. "Discovering the perfect butter tart has been our family's lifelong mission and now Jilly's created it."

Heddy and Kaye sat in the two styling chairs looking impatient and befuddled.

"Ivy, it really wasn't necessary for you to run over here. You had a long day," Kaye said. "We stopped by our store after the celebration and saw your Mom cleaning up in here."

"I don't think I've ever seen Dahlia in jeans," Heddy added, with a smirk.

"I don't think I have either," I said, taking a mug of hot tea from Mom's hand quickly, before they could see her hand shake.

Keats positioned himself between the styling chairs and the rest of us. His ruff was up and his ears back, a definite failing grade for the sisters Langman. Percy, who'd previously been so charming, now sat on the shelf above them puffed to about twice his normal size. His twitching tail suggested he'd fling himself down if needed. His seductive behavior in their shop had clearly been an act.

"Never mind my jeans," Mom said, sounding more confident already. "Chief Harper gave us the go ahead to reopen and someone has to clean this place up. Iris is on her way to pitch in."

"Mom, we'll all help," I said. "I sent out a family SOS. Anyone with free hands will be here in minutes to help clean. Asher's coming, and Kellan too."

The sisters struggled to slide out of the chairs, which Mom had pumped too high.

"Ladies, don't leave," she said. "I was going to give you both some styling tips."

"Another time," Heddy said, zipping her parka. "But we did want to ask you about the so-called treasure Ivy said you found last week at a rummage sale, or some such."

"Oh yes, the cranberry glass vase," Mom said. "I'd love to sell it to you. It really doesn't fit with my décor at home."

"It would be nice right here," Jilly said, tapping the front counter. "Fresh flowers and butter tarts are the best welcome any client could get."

Kaye shook her head. "There was something else. Ivy mentioned a stacking set of animals. Like a rhinoceros or hippo."

"Or was it a manatee?" I asked Mom. "Were there flippers or hooves?"

"Oh darling, I can't remember. I brought it home on a whim thinking it would be fun for a grandchild. But it seems like Daisy is the only one destined to procreate."

"Don't be hasty," I said. "We all still have time."

She tapped her watch. "Tick tock, Ivy. But maybe Jilly will beat you all."

Heddy gave an exasperated grunt. "Where is this so-called manatee? It sounds like something we might like to pick up. We have a buyer who likes peculiar things like that."

"Oh ladies, I'm so sorry," Mom said. "I already threw it away."

"Threw it away?" the sisters said at the same time. "No!"

"It's just junk. If you're really interested, I tossed it in the dumpster behind the grocery store last night. I leave trash there all the time. I love the hunt but I can't stand clutter. It's probably just as well or there'd be no room for me in the apartment."

Heddy and Kaye elbowed each other to get through the door first. They were already in their car before Asher and Kellan arrived, and my sisters straggled in after that, one by one.

"Well, thanks for the speedy emergency response, girls," Mom said, hoisting herself into her barber chair. "Iris, I need to recline."

My sister adjusted the chair so that Mom was practically horizontal. She fanned Mom with one hand while Jilly came over with tea. Mom pretended to be as weak as a kitten, allowing Jilly to tilt up her head and pour a little orange pekoe between her scarlet lips. She may have dressed down but her lips were still dressed up.

"What's going on?" Kellan said.

"It was a butter tart 911," Iris said. "It's the family safe word."

"I get the concept. Asher explained on the way over." He looked at me. "You texted my personal phone so it's obviously not a true emergency."

"It might have been," I said. "But I only needed my, uh —" I hesitated to use the word in front of everyone.

"Boyfriend?" Kellan said, grinning.

"Family," Jilly said, also grinning. "We're honorary Galloways now, Kellan."

He blew out a breath through pursed lips before saying, "Heaven help us, Jilly."

"Right? Never a dull moment with this bunch," she said.

"So what was so important you needed to call for butter tarts, Mrs. Galloway?" Kellan asked.

She lifted her head and glared at him. "Ms. Galloway. I already told you that, Kellan. Since this is a personal call, you may even call me Dahlia."

That would never happen. Or at least not till way down the road, perhaps if we produced that grandchild to play with the imaginary manatee. Where my mother was concerned, Kellan had to juggle professional frustration and personal intimidation. It was kind of fun to watch.

Keats thought so, too. His spirits were high now and he prepared to cut Kellan from the herd of people and bring him in to me.

"Keats," Mom said. "I see you. And I'd really like all the

attention for myself, if you don't mind. I've had a terrible shock."

Kellan moved against a wall so that the dog couldn't circle him. "Thanks for the warning, Ms. Galloway. Now, what happened?"

"Ivy set me up, that's what happened," Mom said. "She told the Langman sisters that I found a rare artifact at a rummage sale. As if I would ever go to a rummage sale, let alone pick up a hippo or a manatee."

"Ah," Kellan said. "You were trying to bait out the Langmans to see if they'd bite."

"And they tried to," Mom said. "They wanted to bite and it wasn't butter tarts they fancied."

"Ivy." Kellan's voice was serious but it was hard to take him seriously when he had backed into a corner to avoid little lunges by Keats that were intended to flush him out. "If you thought one or both of the Langman sisters killed Portia, do you really think it was wise to tell them your mom had a valuable collectible in her possession?"

"I told them it was no longer in her possession when I found them poking around my family room this afternoon. They obviously wanted to find out what she did with it."

Mom still had her head up, neck stretched like a turtle's to glare at me. "I can't believe you'd throw me to those old dogs like that."

"They're your age," I said.

"But they look decades older with those haircuts. I never liked those girls in school, but I had to play nice. They're powerful influencers in town."

"You handled yourself great," I said. "Right now they're up to their waists in garbage looking for a wooden manatee that never existed. Kellan can pop down and arrest them."

He actually laughed. "There's such a thing as just

cause, Ivy. I have no evidence the Langmans did anything wrong."

"Other than to come in here without an invitation and scare me," Mom said. "Not to mention exploring Ivy's house on the sly."

"Plus, Keats doesn't like them," I said.

"I can attest to that," Jilly said. "He normally only acts like he did when someone is rotten to the core."

"See?" I turned back to Kellan, who was easing out of the corner. He obviously thought his pant cuffs stood a better chance if the sheep got on the move.

"And this is how he acts when he *likes* someone?" Kellan said, scooting behind Asher.

"Yeah, Chief," Asher said, grinning. "It is. But I'm glad I can cover you, like you've covered me so often."

"You can at least go down there and question the Langmans," I said. "You know Keats has amazing intuition."

"Well, I can't arrest people based on your dog's nose or intuition," he said. "And if you'd asked me, you'd know I already talked to Heddy and Kaye and they have alibis."

"As if they wouldn't lie for each other," I said. "That's what families do."

"Yeah?" he said. "Is that another Galloway code?"

It was as if he'd taken a match to Asher, whose face burned, and the flame passed quickly from one of us to the next, with the notable exception of shameless Poppy.

"We would if we had to," she said.

"But we haven't had to," I said. "Or at least, very rarely. Anyway, those two are acting pretty shady. They know something."

"They want the fake collectible you metaphorically waved under their nose. You know as well as I do that treasure hunters are passionate. But their alibis checked out."

Mom signaled for Iris to raise the barber chair and slid out. "Well, at least I had the presence of mind to send them on a wild goose chase into the rubbish. I hope they stink for weeks."

Jilly looked reproachfully at Asher. "You could drive over with the lights on and embarrass them, at least."

"People like them don't embarrass easily," he said, leaving Kellan to fend for himself against Keats as he sidled up to Jilly. "Are there real butter tarts in there?"

She gave him the tin. "Crushed pumpkin squares. Share them with the Langmans when you help them out of the trash."

Mom shook her head. "On this I agree with the boys. Leave those two to flounder around in that dumpster. Ivy, go down there and get a photo."

"She will not," Kellan said.

"On this I agree with Kellan," I said, echoing Mom's words.

"Fine." She pulled out her phone. "I'm calling the Expositor to send down a reporter."

"Mom, no!" I think I counted all six voices, even Poppy's. It was loud enough for Keats to flinch and Percy to frisk away to another shelf and start knocking products off deliberately. The first splat of conditioner hitting the hardwood redirected Mom's attention nicely.

"Stop that, you cur," she yelled up at him.

"Only a dog can be a cur," I said.

"Go home, Ms. Galloway," Kellan said. "It's not safe here until we know who killed Portia."

"But you said we could reopen next week."

"Which is not the same thing as being here alone cleaning in the evening."

Putting her hands on her hips, she said, "You don't understand what this—"

"I understand I'm the one driving you home tonight. Can you see yourself home, Ivy? Before I make your brother impound your truck for being parked on the sidewalk?"

"Come on, Keats," I said, deliberately letting the dog take one last dive at Kellan. As I walked past my mother I said, "Enjoy your ride home, Mom."

She tapped her watch at me, getting the last word without saying a thing. Tick tock.

CHAPTER TWENTY-TWO

W e were almost back at the farm when our phones pinged at once. I knew what that meant, even before Jilly pulled out her phone and announced, "Rescue 911."

"Chow chow?" I asked, slowing carefully. Making a U turn here with the truck would be a death wish. I'd need to find a side street or driveway and even then the chances of stalling were high.

Knowing that, Jilly braced herself on the dash as she checked her phone again. "No. The old Bingham manor."

"Huh. Well, at least that's closer than Dorset Hills." It took me a few minutes to find a good place to turn, and then there was a stall midway down the manor lane. I added one more for good measure just before parking.

Cori was doubled over with laughter when the four of us jumped out. "You are a hazard to humans and animals, Ivy Galloway."

"Well, I've saved more lives than I've taken," I said, waving to Bridget, Remi and Andrea MacDuff, who went by Duff. "At least, so far."

Keats trotted over to Cori and offered an elaborate play pose. It was like he was bowing to royalty, which only irritated me more.

"Good," she said. "You brought reinforcements. We need a sheepdog to help with our task."

Keats pranced around her now, awaiting instruction. It was as if he knew that on a Rescue Mafia mission, Cori was top dog.

"What's happened?" I asked.

"When we emptied the manor—off the record, of course —we set up motion activated cameras to let us know if any of Portia's cats were outside."

She offered her phone and Jilly and I looked at the footage. "That's Panther," I said. "Edna's favorite cat. She wanted to keep him."

"Keep watching," Cori said.

On video, Panther came out of the bushes and sat in plain view of the camera, his eyes glowing in the light. Next came a pure white cat. It was Fleecy, who used to belong to one of the Bridge Buddies, but had apparently sworn allegiance to Edna's feral colony. Six or more cats joined them, two of whom looked like my former barn cats. They lined up in a row and sat with their tails wrapped around them. It looked like a pose for a family portrait.

"Oh no," I said. "They've been on their own for days. I stopped putting out food at Edna's after foxes ripped the wire fencing. I guess they migrated over here."

"I think they've been here for awhile," Cori said. "I spotted movement more than once but couldn't get a bead on them. It's like they didn't want to be discovered till now."

"Why now?" I asked. "Because they're finally hungry enough?"

Cori shrugged. "I don't speak cat, and you do. So call them out and let's have a discussion."

"They're not going to come if I call. They're cats."

"You don't know unless you try," she said.

"Fine. Whatever." I took a deep breath and shouted, "Here, kitty-kitty-kitty."

We waited for a few moments and nothing happened, except that Cori laughed, which I expected.

"You're not going to give up that easily, are you?" Cori asked.

"Nope. If you'll surrender your hold on my dog, I'll deploy him and the cat."

"I shouldn't have to surrender him," she said. "If you have to work that hard for his attention, something's undermined your bond."

"What? Keats, come."

He did, but he kept looking back at Cori, as if hoping she'd take over.

"He hung off your every word when we first met," Cori said. "Now he's not. What's happened between you?"

My stomach seemed to curl in on itself and bile rose in my throat. Losing Keats—losing his respect and love—was my worst nightmare. Even with Jilly, Kellan and my family, I was quite sure that would kill me. Or at least kill any desire to live. I'd be nothing more than a shell.

"Relax," Cori said. "You look like you're going to heave."

Remi stepped forward with Leo and tried to force the beagle on me, but I declined. "Cori," she said. "It's a terrible thing to make someone afraid of losing her dog's love. You've done it to me before."

I backed away, still staring at Keats, who was staring at Cori.

"It's a trainer's job to point out changes and prevent that from ever happening," Cori said. "When the cat came along, did you stop listening to Keats, Ivy?"

"No. But he's stopped wanting to come along with me everywhere. If Jilly stays on the farm, he wants to stay. I asked the vet to look him over and he's fine."

"Of course he's fine. But he wants to stay on the farm for a reason. You need to figure out what that is. And the cat is an obvious place to start."

"You said yourself that they're pals," I argued.

"They are pals. Keats likes the cat, but the bond he craves is with you. When we first met, you two were talking your private language all the time and now he's just... a regular dog." Keats offered a whine at that. "A brilliant sheepdog, but within normal parameters. Before, he was extraordinary because the two of you were more than the sum of your parts."

"We've had a lot going on," Jilly said. "And it's cumulative stress. PTSD, more like. Go easy on Ivy."

"I don't go easy," Cori said. "Not my style, because it doesn't benefit anyone."

"She doesn't," Remi said. "Trust me."

"Cori means well," Bridget said. "And this is just something for you to consider. If you feel like all is right between you and Keats, just ignore it."

"I... I know it's not all right. I just don't know how it's wrong. Or how to fix it."

Cori gave a nod of what seemed like grudging approval. "Admitting there's a problem is halfway to fixing it. Just give him your full attention like you used to, and he'll let you know."

I didn't even realize tears were rolling down my cheeks until Keats turned from Cori and nudged my hand. I couldn't see his warm brown eye in the darkness but I felt it filling me up.

"See?" Bridget said. "It's better already."

"It's a start," Cori said. "But with the way you carry on, Ivy, you need that dog working at peak capacity. If you put yourself in harm's way without the magic you two have, you may not come out on top the next time."

"That's enough," Jilly said, moving in front of me.

Cori held up both gloved hands and the neon middle fingers gleamed in the light of Duff's phone. "Peace, pit bull friend. I appreciate your loyalty, but this puts you at risk, too."

"It's okay, Jilly," I said, patting her back. "She's not wrong. I told you something was off."

"You'll fix it," Cori said. "I have complete faith in you, and I don't say that often."

"She doesn't," Remi said. "In fact, I've never heard it."

"And you won't as long as you're singing lullabies to Leo," Cori said. "Now can you get the crates, Remi? Because our feline friends have joined us."

While we were arguing about Keats, Percy had apparently lured his old pals from their hiding spots. He sat at the end of their row now. When Remi and Duff lined up the open crates on the grass, the so-called feral cats stepped inside, one by one, until the only loose feline was Percy.

Cori picked up two crates and loaded them into the bed of my pickup.

"Why my truck?" I asked.

"Two of them are yours, so here's your chance to woo them to stay." She put two more crates in my truck. "Take the others back to Edna's and feed them until she gets home."

"Is that what they want? Or will they just come back here?"

She stared at me in the darkness. "You tell *me* what they want."

I thought about it for a minute while watching Percy race away across the wet grass. "They want a ride home to Edna's. They were here to give their pals moral support but their job is done."

Cori tapped her head with her gloved index finger. "That's using your noggin. And what are *your* pets saying now?"

Keats had run off after Percy and I followed them with my phone light on. The dog was in the garden flinging up dirt between his white paws. "Keats, leave it," I said. "You'll get filthy."

Meanwhile, Percy was nowhere in sight, until my scanning flashlight caught his eyes overhead. It was the old tree house Michael Bingham had loved so much. I wanted to explore it, and I sensed I should, but with a structure that old, it would be better done in daylight.

"Message received," I told them, snapping my fingers and walking back to the others. "We'll be back. For now, we have passengers to deliver."

"See you soon, I hope," Remi said, squeezing my arm. "Everything's going to be fine. I know it."

"Of course it is," Cori said, hopping behind the wheel of her own pickup. She looked like a doll in the large vehicle. "Sometimes we all need a little wake-up call. Even me."

"Did anyone record that?" Remi asked, and they all laughed as they climbed into Bridget's van.

Cori led the convoy out, but when I stalled my truck, she flashed her lights a few times—probably to signal her hilarity—and kept on going.

CHAPTER TWENTY-THREE

Jilly and I released the barn cats into the empty stall and left them with food and water before heading up to the house to check on our guests.

We found Caroline on the couch in the family room working on the needlepoint that seemed to be her constant companion. I sensed it was as therapeutic as my manure pile, only a whole lot cleaner.

She looked up and smiled when she saw us. "I have something to show you," she said, biting off a thread and tucking the needle into the taut fabric.

I took the ring she handed me and a grin spread across my face. "It's Runaway Farm! How lovely."

"I'll have it framed and send it to you when I'm done," she said, rising from the couch. "I might even include Keats, if he'll agree to pose for me."

The dog was pacing back and forth, making a show of brushing my shins. He obviously wanted to get on with the next stage of our evening's mission.

"I'm sure he will tomorrow," I said, knowing that was

unlikely. Posing was probably on par with a bath in the dog's eyes.

"We're leaving to meet friends in Dorset Hills for drinks soon, anyway," she said, turning around. Her dress was only half-zipped. "Would you mind, Ivy? Michael's still in the shower."

I tried to step around Keats and nearly tripped. My arms pinwheeled and I almost clipped Caroline in the head. That was no way to impress a guest.

"I've got it," Jilly said, sidestepping the dog to do as Caroline asked. "Since you and Michael are going out, I can give Ivy a hand."

"You two work so hard. I get tired just watching you," Caroline said, collapsing on the couch again. She unfurled a long strand the exact shade of my red barn, and bit that off, too. "And yet you're always so calm."

I laughed, as Keats parked himself on my boots. "We're like ducks—all glide on the surface while the feet paddle like mad underneath."

"Truth," Jilly said, taking a few steps toward the door.

Caroline laughed, too, as she deftly threaded her needle. "I'm the same way, I guess. When my hands aren't busy."

Maybe she was the one I'd heard pacing the night before. I'd assumed it was Michael, with his boundless energy.

Jilly clapped her hands now. "Ivy, let's get moving. I won't be truly calm until we get this next task out of the way."

"What is it this time?" Caroline asked, jabbing the fabric.

"More barn chores," Jilly called back. "Never ending, never glamorous."

"Also truth," I said, easing my boots out from under Keats. "But you'll make farm life look pretty, right?"

"Of course," she called after me. "Thanks to you two, I only see the pretty, anyway."

I followed Jilly out and then poked my head back in. "Thanks, Caroline. That's the nicest thing a guest has ever said to us."

"YOU'VE LET what Cori said get under your skin, haven't you?" Jilly asked, during the short drive to Edna's.

"Is it that obvious?" I asked.

"Well, you've stalled more than usual and you keep looking at Keats like you don't know him. I haven't heard you say a word to him, other than basic sheepdog business."

"So in other words, normal."

"Right. And you two are far from normal."

"Not you too, Jilly," I said, easing the truck into Edna's lane. "I don't think I can handle another lecture. I feel... broken."

"You're not broken, you're distracted and stressed. It's bad enough when your own livelihood is on the line, but now it's your mom's and Iris's, too." She sighed before adding, "It's cumulative, like I told Cori."

"How could Keats and I get so off kilter that Cori noticed before I did?"

"You did notice. You've brought it up to me several times and had him looked over by a vet."

It was true. I'd seen Senna York twice in three days and asked her to check him each time. She pronounced Keats to be "as fit as a fiddle." Portia Parson, on the other hand, had been far from it, in the veterinarian's opinion. She'd only learned of the cat overpopulation days before The Cat Lady's demise and was trying to come up with a solution that wouldn't stress Portia out more. She never got the chance to intervene.

I glanced at the dog in the back seat and sighed. "Something is off with Keats. I know it, and you know it. I guess I just figured it would fix itself. Maybe I need to rehome—" I jerked my thumb in the direction of Percy, who was lounging against the dog's side. On cue the cat raised huge, glowing eyes. "So that things can go back to normal."

Jilly craned around, too. "Keats and Percy are practically curled up together, and I caught them snuggling in the dog bed yesterday when you were out. The problem isn't the cat."

"Then what is it? I feel like he's... distant. Like a radio station I can't quite tune into." I hit the brakes so fast the truck stalled right beside the pig pool—the deep swampy pond where bad things happened. The timing couldn't be a coincidence. It must be a sign.

"What's wrong?" Jilly asked.

"What if it's me? What if my concussion is finally healing and I can't connect with Keats anymore?"

Jilly actually laughed. "You've told me dozens of times that you wished you could recover fully. So now you don't want that?"

I thought about it for a second, stalled in the dark lane by the treacherous pig pool. "I don't want that anymore, actually. I like being who I am now—the quirky farmer who talks to her animals and believes they talk back in their own way." She let me ponder some more and I added, "I mean it would be good if the headaches went away and I regained some impulse control. But I don't want to give up the rest. It would be like seeing life in black and white again. I can't go back to old Ivy."

She reached out and put her hand over mine as I clutched the steering wheel hard. "I don't think there's any risk of your becoming Old Ivy again. And I'm glad about that because New Ivy is endlessly fascinating and her big heart cracked right open."

"I can't go back. I can't go back..." I muttered. It felt like I was stuck in a nightmare loop that had no way out.

"Stop that right now or I will get out of this truck, risk my life passing the pig pool and open your door to slap you properly."

A long white muzzle poked between the seats and rested on my shoulder. Keats licked my cheek and mumbled something motivational.

"Thank you," I whispered. "Thank you, buddy."

"What did he say?" Jilly asked.

"That he trusts me," I said, starting the truck again and rolling forward. "That it'll work out fine. And that I should get moving."

"See? What did I tell you?" She turned and looked at the dog. "Took you long enough. You can't give her the silent treatment forever, dude." Keats licked her cheek, too. But she wasn't done ranting. "I mean, it's a wonder we keep going at all, yet here we are. Delivering feral cats in the dark to an empty house. How did our lives become so weird?"

"Life is about to become even weirder," I said. "Because the house is neither dark nor empty."

"IVY GALLOWAY! Where are my cats, dagnabit?"

Edna's big old suitcase was still on the porch and she

came out the front door and put her hands on her hips. She was wearing a tweed coat that looked new and her hair, which had been gray when she left, was now dyed tan to match the coat. Even her lines had faded. The Edna who left a few weeks ago had come back a changed woman. At least on the surface.

She stomped down the steps as we got out of the truck, still fuming. "Can't I leave you with a simple task without it getting royally messed up? I saw you stalling that truck in the lane, by the way. Some things never change."

"Like your foul mood, apparently," I said. "And for your information, looking after your feral colony was no simple task. Someone stole most of them before she got murdered in my mom's new salon."

That actually shut her up. It took something extreme to stop Edna Evans, octogenarian and apocalyptic prepper. We had joked that she was impossible to kill, but she was also impossible to beat in verbal warfare. I should know. I had tried often enough. But I'd grown to enjoy our sparring and she'd been letting me win in the week before her trip. I was actually glad her pilot light was back on and spitting fire.

"Who got murdered now?" Edna said. "And why didn't anyone tell me?"

"Most people still aren't speaking to you, for starters," I said. "Some are mad you got murdered and others are mad you didn't. Either way, they felt duped."

"Don't get smart with me, young lady. I will box your ears, just as I did your brother before he got all high and mighty. You've sent me plenty of emails that neglected to mention either missing cats or murders."

"We didn't want to ruin your trip, Edna," Jilly said. "You deserved some down time."

Edna gave Jilly the once-over, ending with a scornful sneer at the pajamas and rubber boots. She hadn't bothered to change when we were home.

"I don't need to hear from you yet, Jillian," Edna said. "The one with the murder problem is Ivy."

I shook my head. "As I recall, the most recent murder problem was yours, Edna."

"And now it's yours again, as one would expect. Someone's dead, yet it wasn't worth mentioning. Typical." She shook herself and looked around. "It's good to be home."

"Are you drunk, Edna?" I asked. "Were they handing out tangerine vodka on the plane?"

"I wish. There was so much turbulence I wanted to throw the captain out of the cockpit and take over. Honestly. He looked sixteen years old." She paused for breath and stared at me. "Well...? Where are my cats and who died?"

"There's good news and there's bad news. First—"

"Get to the point, Ivy. I'm over eighty and might not live long enough for you to finish beating around the bush."

"Fine. In a nutshell, Portia Parson stole your cats and then someone killed her."

"Portia? Why on earth would she steal my cats? Did she lose her mind? Why, I'd kick her across hill country and back if she weren't already dead."

"We don't have all the answers yet, but in a way, yes, she did lose her mind. She thought these animals were suffering and moved most of them into the Bingham manor."

Edna came down the stairs and walked to the passenger side of the truck. "Let's go and get them right now."

Resting my arms on the hood, I said, "Edna, I'm sorry. Most of them are gone. For good."

All the fire vanished and she looked 80 again. "Gone for good? Did the County...?"

"No! I have friends who rescued them and placed them in shelters. Many have been successfully adopted already. We raised money to help."

She stared at me with eyes that were dark holes in the light streaming from the porch. "All gone? Fifty of them?"

"No, no! I mean yes, that's the good news." I ran around the truck and pulled Panther's crate from the back. When I released him, he ran over to Edna and wove around her flesh-colored support hose and sensible oxford lace-ups.

By the time she'd bent over to pat him, I'd released Fleecy and the two remaining gray tabbies.

Standing, she brushed at her eyes. "Let Red out of the truck, too."

"He's adopted us, I'm afraid. His name is Percy."

"Percy. Oh, lord, not another romantic poet. He deserves better than that."

I opened the door and Percy leapt down. He circled Edna's legs in a tight figure eight and then came to sit on my boots.

"You see?" I said. "He and Keats have hit it off."

She shrugged. "Fine. As long as I have visiting rights."

"He's free to come and go as he likes," I said, smiling. This had all gone far better than expected. Four cats were plenty, when all was said and done, and now Edna didn't need to worry about placing the others.

"Who's that?" she said, turning at a crackle in the bush down the lane. "Someone's on my property. Eavesdropping." Stomping toward the sound she called, "Don't make me go inside for my gun, whoever you are."

"Edna, you can't shoot anyone." I ran after her, but Keats beat me to it and herded her gently back.

Down the lane, we heard an engine turn over.

Edna shook off my arm. "You know what? I'm done with playing the nice guy. We're going after him."

"We're what?"

She shoved me out of the way and hurried to the truck. "Get while the getting's good, ladies, because I'm driving."

"This is my truck," I said, jostling with her at the driver's door.

"Tell that to the dang truck," she said, giving me a sharp elbow in the ribcage. "Leave the driving to someone who knows how to use a stick, for pity's sake."

"You are out of line, Edna," I said, blocking her next blow.

"While you're getting butt hurt, the creeper's getting away," she said. "It's Portia's killer, mark my words."

There was a mad scramble as we all got into the truck, with Jilly and the animals in the back, and me in the passenger seat. Before my door was even closed, Edna gunned it down the driveway. She rolled down the window and let out a whoop.

"Slow down! Are you crazy?" I shouted over Jilly's shrill scream as we rounded a tight curve at breakneck speed.

Edna stuck her head out the window and hollered. "Coming for you, loser. Better hurry."

There wasn't a single hiccup as we pursued a beat-up old brown car into town. I had to hand it to Edna: she knew how to handle a truck and she was good with a tail. She gained on the brown car fast, and if she hadn't gotten cocky and tried to run it off the road in front of the recreation center, things would have ended much differently. Instead, she gained the attention of a passing police car, and the sirens and flashing light came on. I thought she was going to flee, but she knew when to call it. Still, the language as she pulled over and saw Kellan getting out of the SUV was a little spicy.

"Talk him down, Ivy," she said. "I can't afford demerit points."

"You don't even own a vehicle," I said.

"I do now. I'm buying your truck for a fair price so you can get something you can actually handle."

I put my face in my hands. "As if I don't get into enough trouble on my own... Now Kellan's caught me joyriding with a feisty octogenarian, a dog, a cat and poor Jilly."

"There was no joy in that ride," Edna said, rolling up the window. "Get your story straight. I saw a trespasser and pursued. It's likely he was after the last of my cats and I will defend what is mine."

Kellan knocked on the glass. Then he leaned over and his mouth dropped open when he saw who was driving. Keats whined and clawed at the glass in the back to get at him.

Edna put her hand on the window button and then chuckled. "For the record, I lied. There was plenty of joy in that ride."

CHAPTER TWENTY-FOUR

The next day I doubled down on farm work, spending considerable time on my manure pile to ground myself after the mayhem of the previous day. I could handle some mayhem but was no fan of roller coasters. Yesterday had been one heck of a wild ride, from the celebration of Portia's life, through rescuing Mom from the Langman sisters, to getting chastised by Cori Hogan during the Rescue Mafia 911, and finally the car chase with Edna at the wheel. To round things off, I got a second lecture of the day from Kellan, and a thorough razzing from Edna about my driving as I took her home.

If it weren't for the guests, I'm sure Jilly and I would both have gone back to bed after breakfast. Michael was at loose ends. Hazel had warned me her nephew bored easily and they were set to depart the next day. In the meantime, Jilly and I offered a list of activities that might engage them. Michael surprised me by taking up Jilly's suggestion of joining her for a full-day cooking class in Dorset Hills, that would be followed by dinner in the city's best restaurant. It was good of her, because she could actually be teaching cooking classes to others.

Caroline wasn't interested in learning to cook and after sweetly turning down every other suggestion, opted to spend the day with needlepoint and napping. As close as she was to Michael, she probably craved some "me time." He was constantly on the go, a true extrovert, whereas she often went an entire meal without saying a word, other than to prompt him to share his stories. It was a perfect example of how very different personalities could complement each other. I liked to think Kellan and I had some of that working for us, what with his steady, serious focus and my more spontaneous, irrepressible curiosity.

On the other hand, he'd described my behavior the night before as impulsive and dangerous. Edna had started it, but I'd gone along with it. He'd ended the discussion by questioning her faculties and mine. It was the opposite of romantic.

"Oh Keats," I said, as I dug deep with my spade and turned the manure. "Relationships are hard at the best of times. Relationships with murder in the mix are... well, murder."

He mumbled something at me from the base of the pile. Instead of patrolling and surveying his charges, the dog stayed with me. Occasionally, he flicked his eyes at Percy, who was aggravating the camelids simply by sitting on a post in their pasture and twitching his tail. It was provoking the donkeys, who gathered nearby to plot their next move.

Normally, Keats would interrupt Percy's game. He may not like either the donkeys or the llamas, but he still liked order on his farm. The cat was a disruptor, just for the sake of it. He was bored, too.

"Percy, go entertain yourself elsewhere," I called. "Try hunting like a normal cat."

The orange tail flicked harder and reminded me of Cori Hogan's signature gloves.

Keats changed position, ears pricked and head constantly swivelling. I got the sense he was guarding his domain from something, but had no idea what. Later, I'd send Charlie around on the tractor to see if there were any signs of intruders, human or otherwise.

"Keats?" He glanced up at me for a second. "I apologize for not listening to you lately. I think it's a combination of me being distracted and you choosing to stay on the farm instead of riding with me. But let that end today. You have my undivided attention, and I'd love to have yours. I feel like we're on the verge of something big."

He mumbled and it sounded like agreement. Anxious agreement, but I'd take what I could get.

"Let's take a walk to clear our heads. The next steps are circling like turkey vultures in the periphery of my mind. I can't get them to land if I don't give them space."

The dog got up and started pacing, as if torn. Normally the prospect of a walk had him dancing on white paws like a dressage horse. Well, now was the time to listen.

"What do you think we should do, buddy? Walk or farm work? I'll follow your lead."

He went back and forth a few more times, nose up, sniffing for threats. Finally he started walking toward the meadow and looked back with a clear message: "You coming?"

Out in the fields, we climbed the small hill that let me look down over the farm and Edna's house. My spirits rose and I sucked in the fresh air as if I hadn't had any for weeks.

Keats was still a bit jumpy, but after a mile or so, he flushed Percy out of the brush and gave chase with jubilant barking. Now I sighed with relief. My dog was still in there, and his mood had nothing to do with the cat.

There was a big rock at the top of the hill that glaciers had dropped eons ago. I climbed up and sat with Keats on one side and Percy on the other. After a spell of quiet contemplation, Keats gave me a nudge with his muzzle and then turned in the direction of town. I shifted to follow his gaze and saw nothing but gently rolling meadows and trees desperately clinging to a few bright leaves, like scraps of clothing. Somewhere in between sat the Bingham manor but I couldn't see it from here.

Keats whined and poked me again. This time he stared up at me with his eerie blue eye and didn't shift his gaze until I said, "How about we head over to the manor? See if we missed anything?"

He jumped up and now the dressage horse paws came into action. Percy also left his silent reflection and the two jostled to be first down the hill, although there was plenty of open space for all of us.

"Boys, boys," I said. "Can't we all just get along?"

All the way back they frolicked, stopping only when I got out my phone to make a call.

"Okay," I said. "So I know what we're looking for now. But I'm going to have to count on you two to help me find it. Understood?"

Percy took a flying leap and landed right on the dog's back. Keats let out a startled yelp and as the cat spring-boarded off, gave chase. They were soon out of sight, and I enjoyed the rest of the descent alone, only to find them both sitting beside the truck when I got home. Buttercup had been towed into town for service while we were gone, so it was either the truck or the golf cart, which were sitting side by side.

Keats voted with his paws on the door of the pickup.

"Stalling it is," I said, pulling out my keys. "Remember, you asked for it."

As we drove to the manor, I said, "I've decided not to sell Edna the truck. It's tempting but that would be admitting failure. And worse, admitting failure to Edna. I've just got a mental block about the pickup and I've solved many a bigger mental block. So, just as soon as we get Portia's murder sorted, I'm taking those lessons I've cancelled five times. It's a matter of pride." After a minute I added, "And fear. I honestly think Kellan will dump me if there's another episode like last night. His reputation is on the line. It must be so embarrassing for him to have me stalling around town. Then I surrendered the wheel to Edna and participated in a car chase... well, that may have been the last straw. I couldn't blame him."

Keats mumbled something and I turned to see him happy-panting.

"Fine, it wasn't the *last* straw. But when it comes to his job, he probably only has a few straws and I'm using them up fast."

Keats stood up against the dashboard and I said, "Why do I get the distinct impression we're going to use another straw or two today?"

Percy let out a meow from the back that prompted me to pick up the pace. I missed Jilly riding shotgun on this one, but it felt good to have unity with my pet partners in crime. Or crime-solving.

After a pretty much flawless drive, I pulled up in front

of the manor and parked. Now the sun was starting its downward slide into the trees, although it was barely four p.m. I'd intended to make this trip the next morning after the guests left. But now I was following Keats' lead and today was obviously the day.

"Alright," I said, jumping down. "Fan out, boys. We're looking for the security camera the police couldn't find. Maud Burnett at the central post office confirmed Portia received one a few weeks ago. She chose not to have it shipped through Mandy's Country Store, so she was keeping this quiet. But I'm betting it's here somewhere and that's how she knew we peeped on her that night. Honestly, I can't blame her. With Silvio the butcher coming by to threaten her and people breaking her windows, she was right to worry. It wasn't just paranoia."

I walked around the house, evaluating the best sight lines. If I were trying to monitor this place, I'd have two or even three cameras, placed high enough to see all movement on four sides.

Thinking back, I realized Percy had given me a clue the night before. And sure enough, when I turned, he was up in the tree house again.

Walking to the base of the old "ladder," I cringed. "Oh no. These are just sticks hammered into the tree and they're decades old. It's fine for you Percy, but they look like they're rotting out. I wish I'd brought a ladder."

Keats ran back to the truck and barked.

"Right," I said. "Rope. Good thinking."

At some point I'd thrown a good length of nylon line into the back in case one of the animals escaped, or we came upon another rescue. Now it came in handy in another way. It took half a dozen tosses before I finally got it looped over a branch above the tree house and used my phone to look up how to tie it off properly. Then I knotted it around my waist. It wouldn't be pleasant swinging from this rope—I might squish a few organs—but it was better than coming down the harder way.

The best part about the rope was that it cut my fear by half as I slowly and carefully scaled the old ladder Michael had probably scampered up in his childhood. Finally I hoisted myself onto the platform and sat for a moment to catch my breath. I could see why this place held such warm memories for that lonely boy of long ago. It had a commanding view of both the front and two sides of the house. He would have had complete privacy to create his imaginary world while his mother and aunt talked about their eccentric brother.

Percy was sitting on the ledge of one of the three walls. He reached down and swatted at my hair.

"Right, moving on." After checking that the boards were solid, I stood. "Where is it, Percy?"

He traipsed along the ledge without a care in the world. No tying off needed for this athlete.

At the front, looking over the house, he braced his paws on a broad tree and meowed.

"This one?" I leaned out to get a look around the trunk. "Oh no. No no no."

Percy meowed again. A definitive yes. Above us, there was a hole in the tree, created either by a boy long ago or another critter. It wasn't fresh, but it did look like the perfect place for a security camera.

Even with the rope, this maneuver was going to be tricky. I'd have to climb onto the slim edge of the tree house wall that looked barely wide enough for Percy's orange paws. Then I'd have to reach inside the hole and hope I didn't record a spectacular fall for posterity.

Rubbing my hands through my hair, I thought hard but couldn't come up with another solution, other than calling out a cherry picker.

I looked down and saw Keats staring up. The white tuft of his tail swished once. Affirmative.

"Fine," I said, carefully hoisting myself into a sitting position on the edge. "Don't look down. Eye on the prize."

Standing took more courage—and flexibility—than I thought I had. Thank goodness I'd worn sneakers instead of my usual work boots. I pivoted to hug the tree for dear life with my left arm and reached up and into the hole with my right.

"Bingo," I said, when my fingers touched cool metal. I groped around a little to get a sense of its dimensions, and then... "What the heck?"

A minute later, I'd pulled not one camera but two from the hole in the tree. Both looked relatively new, and one was small and no doubt high end.

"Why didn't I bring a bag or something?" I said, slipping the larger camera into the kangaroo pouch on my overalls. The smaller one I tucked into my bra. It was the only way to keep them from clanking together and possibly damaging the footage during the climb down.

The relief flooding through me made getting down even harder than getting up. It felt like my arms and legs had become limp spaghetti and I nearly took a spin on that rope twice.

Percy had disappeared over the side before I even started, so I was surprised he wasn't waiting at the bottom. Neither was Keats.

"Boys!" I called. "What are you... *Keats!* Stop that digging. What did I tell you— Oh. Oh my gosh! Is that a—?"

My scream startled the dog and he struggled to regain his balance for a second. But he didn't drop the femur—the longest bone in the human body—as he ran toward me.

CHAPTER TWENTY-FIVE

"Drop it. Drop it!"

Keats had already dropped the bone, so he looked up at me questioningly. Now it was really more about what to do with it.

The first thing was to get it off my sneakers. Obviously. I slid one foot out from under the bone and then nudged it gently off the other. I didn't know who this femur had belonged to, but it was best to assume the person deserved some dignity and respect until I learned otherwise.

"Keats, show me the rest," I said, gesturing to the garden where he'd been digging. It wasn't much of a garden, and probably hadn't been for decades. There was a huge prickly rose bush that had somehow bloomed last summer despite— or perhaps because of—the circumstances. I knew a lot about fertilizer now, but this particular brand seemed too old to be feeding the roses. Unfortunately, I also had experience with old bones from the circumstances around meeting Keats. His horrible former owner had buried someone under the sunflowers in the backyard. The dog had unearthed a skull and things spiralled out of control after that, leaving me with both the pup and a concussion.

Now Keats had uncovered another skeleton, it seemed. If it hadn't been my second rodeo, I don't think I could have looked into the hole he'd dug. There was only so much even a manure-friendly farmer could take.

On first glance—and it was going to be my only glance—it appeared that the rest of the individual in question resided under the rose bush as well. My thoughts were as scattered as the bones seemed to be, so I looked up at the sky and pulled in a breath to the count of nine. If I could have made it to 19 it still wouldn't have calmed me. Nine would have to do.

Reaching into the pocket of my overalls, I fumbled around the security camera for my phone. Then I snapped a few photos, taking a second or two to get the right light and perspective so that the police could find the remains easily.

In each photo, orange paws busily scratched dirt back over the bones, as if burying something in a large litter box.

"You go, Percy," I muttered. "But now we have to go. It's getting dark."

I jogged to the femur in the dried grass and said, "What do I do with that?" I could put it back where it currently belonged or hide it somewhere. Picking it up, I looked around for a likely spot to conceal it.

That's when I heard a motor in the distance. Not a car or a truck. Perhaps an ATV. Regardless, it was coming our way and it was picking up speed.

"Boys, run," I whispered, tucking the femur under my left arm. I used my right hand to press the cameras against my chest. The delicate technology likely held answers to Portia's demise.

We got to the truck without mishap and never had I been so happy to slide behind the wheel.

"Okay. We're okay," I said. Both animals settled in the back seat, and I realized Keats didn't want to share the front seat with the bone. I didn't either, but there was no help for it. I gingerly placed it in the footwell of the passenger seat and shook off my gloves, muttering another apology. "Sorry, whoever you are. You may be in for another rough ride."

The pickup cooperated rather nicely, considering how jittery I was. Rolling down the window, I managed to turn it around and start down the lane. I put the window down and slowed just enough to hear the vehicle still approaching. It was on the ATV trails Jilly and I had taken not long ago. If I stuck to the lane, I wouldn't run into them, literally or otherwise.

Keeping the lights out, I used my phone to show the way, minimizing the chance that the approaching vehicle would see the truck through the dense bush and change direction. It took a little doing to steer with one hand and light the way with the other and I had to stay in first gear almost to the highway. Only then did I flick on the headlights and gun it as I never had before. It made Edna's wild drive the night before look like a kiddie ride at a theme park.

By the time I reached the police station downtown, I was huffing like I'd run the entire way. Instead, I'd mainly held my breath. I was afraid of stalling, afraid of being tailed and afraid of smelling something worse than manure if I let my nose do its job. Logically I knew that bone was far too old to smell of more than soil but my roiling stomach couldn't be convinced of reason. It wanted to toss the fish tacos Jilly had left for Caroline and me to reheat at lunch. If there was a worse meal than fish before an expedition, I didn't know it.

"Liver, maybe?" I said aloud, and Keats stuck his head through the seats to stare at me. "What? You think I'm losing it, don't you? Well, I'm not. This isn't the first time we've dealt with a skeleton and I can handle it better this time. I ran away from the threat, not toward it, right? Total improvement in my judgement. Here we are at the police station, where I can just drop this stuff off. Then we're all going home to take a long bath."

Keats shuddered and I said, "Well, maybe not you, buddy. It would seem like unfair punishment after some excellent sleuthing." I looked over my shoulder. "You too, Percy. Good job, team."

Shuddering myself, I put my gloves back on and picked up the femur. "I can't just walk in there carrying it, can I?" Keats mumbled a decided negative. "I could trigger some kind of statewide alert. But there's no way I'm leaving it out here. So…" I looked down and sighed. "There goes another perfectly good bag. I lost my favorite to a skull and now its replacement to a femur." Stuffing it in the big leather bag, I said, "A grim reaper farmer just can't have nice things."

I looked around carefully and then opened the door of the truck. "Come on, you two. No way am I leaving you behind, either. Someone's after me and they can take the truck if they want but they're not getting my animals or my femur." I shook my head. "That didn't come out right. But you know what I meant."

Keats panted nervously, herding me up the front steps of the police station. Percy circled me, nearly tripping me at the top with his figure eight weave through my sneakers. It was as if the cat didn't want me to go inside. Yet where else would I go? This made the most sense.

"Come on, hurry," I said, opening the door with one hand and concealing the knobby top of the femur in my armpit. "We'll just find Kellan and drop the goods. Nothing to it."

Only Kellan wasn't waiting to greet me at the front desk, because I hadn't thought to call ahead. Instead, a prim-looking older woman with an elaborate bun stared at me as I walked across the short foyer.

"Can I help you, ma'am?" she asked.

Maybe it was the ma'am that threw me off, or maybe it was the thinly veiled look of contempt. All of a sudden I realized exactly how I must look. It was like I was given an aerial view of farmer Ivy in her overalls, bulky with a camera in one pocket, another in her bra, and the longest bone in the human body tucked into her armpit. My hair was windblown and my makeup streaming from tears I only felt now. On top of all that, I was flanked by a dog on one side and a cat on the other. The latter took the liberty of leaping on the counter in front of the plexiglass and meowing loudly into the speaker.

"Ma'am?" the woman prompted me. "How can I help you?"

"Kellan," I whispered. "I need to see Kellan, please."

"Chief Harper? I'm afraid he's busy, ma'am. And he doesn't take random callers."

"I'm not random," I said. "I'm his girlfriend."

"You're his...?" Her voice trailed off and she shook her head in disbelief.

Percy leaned into the speaker and released a yowl. It was deafening even from my side of the glass. "Percy, stop." He sat back on his haunches and scratched at the glass with both paws, trying to dig his way in.

"Stop that right now," the woman said. "Or I will have you removed."

I didn't know if she meant me or Percy, but I slid my hand under the cat and dropped him gently to the floor.

"Sorry," I said. "If Kellan is busy could you please call my brother? Asher Galloway."

"Oh," she said, recognition dawning. "Are you the Galloway sister with the...?"

Again she trailed off. She was annoying enough that some of my spirit came flooding back, starting around the region of the fish taco and moving up into my chest. "Ma'am," I said, tossing the word back at her, "I'll ask one more time. I need to speak to Chief Harper or Officer Galloway right now. It's an emergency."

"Is that a...?" She picked up the phone quickly with her right hand and pointed with her left. The femur had slipped out of my armpit when I moved Percy, and now it hit the counter with a loud thunk.

"Yes," I said. "It's a femur. The longest bone in the human body. And I'd really like to hand it over to someone better equipped to deal with it than I am."

Percy jumped up to add another meow for punctuation.

But he didn't get to hum many bars before a door to my left opened and two uniformed officers came out.

Neither was Kellan or Asher. Instead, two rather brawny women pretty much picked me up and transported me inside without any need for my sneakers to move. I looked down and saw Keats holding one of them by the cuff with his four white brakes on. Percy took a leap and landed lightly about mid-back on the other. I knew how that felt... exactly like a big burr you couldn't dislodge. Neither woman even slowed down. At some point, there was a rather loud clatter as the femur fell to the floor, but even then they kept on moving. It was like being caught in a tractor beam and I had no idea where it would drop me.

So when Kellan happened to step through a doorway, it's really no wonder that his jaw dropped. "Ivy? What on earth...?"

It was all sentence fragments around here. But I had a complete one for him.

"We found Aaron Bingham."

CHAPTER TWENTY-SIX

"Well. That was certainly embarrassing," I said, putting my boot on the spade and kicking it rather aggressively into the manure pile. It was dark, now, but enough light flooded through the wide double doors of the barn to let me take out my frustrations in the usual way. "I'm pretty sure I'm no better than dung to Kellan now, boys."

Keats and Percy sat together on the side closest to the barn. From my vantage point, they looked like toy soldiers on night watch.

"I can't figure it out," I muttered, tossing manure down the other side. "I should know this. I should know."

Keats glanced up and his eerie blue eye confirmed it. I *should* know by now. He knew.

"What am I missing?" I stuck the spade into the pile, crossed my arms around the handle and stared around.

My eyes fell on the golf cart and suddenly everything fell into place. Because the cart was parked on an angle. Someone had taken it for a ride when I was gone.

"Boys, I hate to tell you this," I said, "But we've got to head back to the police station. Now."

Four eyes stared up at me. Only the brown one didn't glow. They blinked once. They blinked twice.

"Don't say no," I pleaded. "This is our chance to—"

"To do what?"

I jumped and nearly dropped the spade. Caroline Bingham was standing in the rear doorway of the barn wearing a pretty dress and heels. She'd told me earlier that she was joining Michael and Hazel in town for their final dinner. After a long rest and a bath, she looked like a million bucks. Meanwhile I looked little better than the crap I stood on.

"To make things right with Kellan," I said. "I embarrassed him rather spectacularly earlier."

Caroline laughed. "Don't worry. He'll forgive you. I saw the look on his face the other day when he was here. He thinks you're a doll."

I pulled the spade out of the manure and took another savage stab at it. "Not after today. Unless you count that demonic little doll with the red hair. You know the one?"

"Chuckie," she said, laughing again. "I think you're being too hard on yourself. Not to mention the manure pile. You'll excuse me if I stand well back to avoid splatter."

"Of course." I stuck the spade into the pile and leaned on it again. "You look wonderful, Caroline. Michael stares at you as if you're a precious gemstone. In case you hadn't noticed."

She smiled and then it faded. "Sometimes I notice, but then I have doubts. He's such a sweet man. I really don't deserve him."

"Of course you do. Why on earth would you say that? Hazel says she's never heard a single harsh word out of you.

That means something, trust me. I barely get through a day without a harsh word or five."

"You've been under a lot of pressure, Ivy. I couldn't quite believe the stories I heard in town. Hazel never said a word about it, and honestly I'm not sure we'd have stayed here if we'd known what's been happening at Runaway Farm."

"I'm sorry. I guess we should have filled you in but I thought most of the clouds over the farm had passed."

"What I meant to say is that I was grateful we didn't know because we've had the most marvellous time here with you and Jilly. You're wonderful hosts and I promise we'll be referring you far and wide."

"Whew!" I said, forcing a grin. "You had me worried there for a second."

"My only reservation is the dog," she said, looking down.

"The dog?" My eyes dropped, too, and I saw Keats had positioned himself between us. His ruff was up, his ears back and his tail stood straight out. "Oh. That. He must hear a coyote. He's been jumpy all day."

"It's not just today," Caroline said. "Every day he follows me around on tiptoes. He blocks me in rooms and he won't let me get anywhere near Jilly when you're not home. We were just laughing about it yesterday."

"He hasn't been himself lately. I even had the vet check him out, but I'll take him again tomorrow. Maybe there's a thorn in his paw or something. He was limping earlier on our walk."

I didn't call Keats off, though. I knew exactly why he was behaving like that. And it meant I needed help. Fast.

Scooping a generous shovelful of manure, I pulled back and flung it. Not close enough to hit Caroline but sufficiently close to surprise her. She ducked back into the barn and called, "Ivy, watch it. I have dinner plans."

"Sorry! Accident!" I glanced at Percy, who stood on the manure steps with his back arched and tail puffed. "Get help, Percy, please," I hissed. For once, the cat took a direct order and disappeared into the darkness on stealthy paws.

Jilly should be back by now. Michael's change of plans allowed her to come home early, while he went to collect Hazel from Sunny Acres. Reaching into my pocket I was relieved to find my phone. I only had time to hit the record button before Caroline reappeared.

"What was that about?" she asked. "It was like you had a spasm."

With the spade firmly in hand, I came down my stairway to heaven. "Again, I'm so sorry, Caroline. I've had an exhausting day and obviously need to pack it in."

She came through the doorway right into the yard. Now she was carrying the pig poker—the long wooden pole with the iron hook on the end that Charlie and I used to redirect unruly livestock, especially Wilma the pig.

"You hit me, I hit you," she said, still smiling.

I laughed. "No more manure, Caroline, I promise."

"That's a promise you can't keep, Ivy. You live for manure."

There was a shift in the atmosphere, like an electrical storm rolling in. The hair on my arms and the back of my neck rose.

"Jilly says the same thing," I said. "I come here to work out my frustrations, and it's turned into a strange love affair."

"A love affair with manure. That really is strange." She came another few steps toward me. "It won't take you anywhere good, Ivy. In fact, it won't take you anywhere but under. And what a sad way to go."

"Caroline." I tipped my head. "What a strange thing to say. Are you okay?"

"No, I am not okay. I'm in very deep trouble because of you."

"Me! What have I done, other than offer the finest hospitality in hill country?"

"You stuck your nose in where it didn't belong, Ivy. And that can only be because you've destroyed your sense of smell by spending too much time out here."

Keats was still puffed, still providing a fur barrier between us. I wanted to call him off, though, because she might very well knock him out of the way to get to me. She already had a hate on for him and one wrong move would be all it took for her to swing.

"You're right," I said, knowing those words could work like magic on the most deranged individual, and it was starting to look like Caroline was exactly that. "I have gotten myself into trouble over and over lately. It all started with the head injury from saving Keats. Did you know—"

"Jilly told me. She said Keats dug up a skull in his owner's backyard and you confronted the killer with it. I don't know whether to call you brave or stupid."

I pretended to think about it. "Stupid. I own it. That wasn't my smartest decision."

"And yet it paid off for you. Big time. Look at what just fell in your lap." She waved her hand in the direction of the inn. "Some girls have all the luck."

"What do you mean? You and Michael have a wonderful life. Hazel says you're two perfectly matched rolling stones without a care in the world."

"Hazel doesn't know that Michael's never been good

with money. So when she offered the manor to him years ago, he let pride stand in his way, assuming it would come to him down the road anyway. But then she gave it to that disgusting cat lady. I couldn't believe it."

"Oh, poor Michael," I said. "He must have been hurt."

"Not Michael," she said. "He doesn't take things to heart like that. He loves his aunt even though she burned him for trash. That man doesn't have a bad bone in his body."

"He doesn't need to, I guess. He's got you to look out for him."

She nodded. "It's been that way since college. I saw his potential. He's bright, he's charming, and so soft-hearted. What I didn't realize was that he'd give away the farm to anyone in need, leaving us in need ourselves. I always held down a good job, but it wasn't enough. Anyone who came with hand outstretched got it filled by Michael."

"That must have been so frustrating. Working so hard and seeing it frittered away. Even for good causes."

"They weren't always good causes. People exploited him. Took from him. Took from us."

I gradually moved around the manure mound, signaling Keats to stay with me. The goal was to get the pile between us, so that if she struck she'd hit poop. Though I could most certainly outrun those heels, I would not leave her armed and dangerous with my livestock.

All I could do was keep her talking till help arrived. Granted, it was taking longer for that to happen than I'd hoped. I should have given the job to Keats. Cats were unreliable.

"So what happened after Hazel gave the Bingham manor to Portia Parson?" I asked. "You stayed on good terms, so you must not have raised a fuss."

"I kept my mouth shut, like I always do. But I went to talk to Portia about doing the right thing."

"Giving the property to Michael?"

"Exactly. But she wouldn't do it. She said Hazel wanted her to have it and it was her responsibility to care for the place and the cats." She tapped the wooden end of the pig pole on the spongy dirt. "That woman is obnoxious."

"*Was*," I said. "She's gone now. The way is clear for you to take over the house. All you need to do is talk to Hazel. Ownership is reverting to her."

Caroline's eyes lit up for a second. "That's what I hoped. She never discusses it."

"She wants it to stay in the family. It sounds like a win-win to me."

"Except for one thing," Caroline said. "You."

"Me? How am I in the way?"

"You know too much, that's how." She held up her phone. "I saw you climbing in the tree house today. You stuffed my camera down your bra, but there's another one you didn't find."

"Ah. So one of the cameras at Portia's was yours. But what's the problem?"

"The problem is your stupid dog. He dug up Aaron."

"So it *was* Aaron! How did he end up under the rose bush?"

She stared at me for a second and then shrugged. "I pushed him out of the tree house, that's how."

The blatant admission startled me enough that my heart, already racing, kicked into overdrive. I was going to have to be extremely careful in how I handled Caroline if I wanted to buy more time. And I desperately wanted to buy more time. The best way to do that, I figured, was to act nonchalant in a dire situation. Fortunately, I'd had plenty of practice.

"So... Aaron wasn't as sweet as Hazel and Michael said?" I asked.

"Far from it. I barely said a word to him when Michael brought me home in college, but Aaron seemed to hate me on sight. Like your dog. He was just around all the time, watching me. He even tried to talk Michael out of marrying me, which luckily didn't work. You know what Aaron gave us as a wedding present? A teakettle. A stupid, leaky teakettle. Meanwhile he was sitting on a ton of money because of his collectibles. Michael's credit was already so poor we couldn't even think about buying a house without help. So I swallowed my pride and asked Aaron on our next visit if he'd lend us some money. He said no, without even batting an eye. Meanwhile he was pouring thousands into ugly toy circus animals. Selling just two of them could have given us a down payment."

"How did Michael take it?" I asked.

She shook her head, lost in the past. "He never knew. Never will know. The day it happened he'd gone to a family reunion for the weekend with his mom and Hazel. I had a headache, and Aaron certainly made it worse. I tried to prove there were no hard feelings by asking him to show me how he built the tree house. Up we went and then—Oops! Over he went. It was easier than I expected. I already had the hole dug, and then I made it look like he'd gone off on his own trip. It was all perfect except for one thing..."

"And that was...?" Despite the circumstances, I truly was on the edge of my seat.

"I couldn't find his collection. It had been on display in his room before and now it wasn't. I searched high and low before the others got back and nothing. Hazel knew and she'd never say. So every time we visited over all those years, I'd send the two of them out for a nice dinner and search the house. When I heard she'd sold them off, I was furious. That fortune was meant to be Michael's. The collection was worth more than the old house and the land it's built on."

She closed her eyes for a second and I took a few more steps.

"But some pieces are still around," I said. "You must know that."

"Yeah." She advanced again. "Portia thought she'd get in good with the old lady by buying some of them back. She was always borrowing money and searching. Gradually she collected some of Aaron's favorites."

"Hazel never knew, I assume."

Caroline shook her head. "I visited Portia about six months ago, after I heard from other collectors what she was doing. I told her I wanted to buy a piece from her, as a family heirloom for Michael. She refused to sell. It was going to be a surprise for Hazel."

"So you started harassing her. Making her so nervous she looked crazy."

"Indirectly. I have a local connection who'd drop by and poke around when she was out." Caroline shrugged. "You can buy anything online these days. Collectibles and thugs."

"But he couldn't find the art either."

"Not until Portia got so rattled with her cat hoarding that she decided to move the pieces out of the manor. At your mother's salon launch, I saw Portia go downstairs. My hired hand had connections with Robbi Ford and he knew she used to offer storage for a price. So we staked Portia out 24/7 until she made the move. I was grateful to you and your crazy family for not only flushing out the valuables, but picking a fight with Portia, too."

"Glad we could help. Crazy comes in handy sometimes."

"Doesn't it? There was enough to go around, because Portia was falling apart. Getting sloppy. When I followed her to the salon, she left the door unlocked and I went downstairs after her. I had her trapped but she'd already stashed the stuff. We were arguing when your Mom came in and started clomping around upstairs. Portia was in a bind too, having let herself in, and she wasn't thinking straight. I thought she'd fight like a wild cat but she went down in an instant."

"Your embroidery scissors?" I asked.

"They're a good deal at the hardware store in town," she said. "Everyone has them."

Her smile was wide and uncomfortably familiar. I'd seen madwomen before, unfortunately.

"But how did you get out? There's no exit."

"You kept your mom nicely distracted talking about rats and quality tissues, and I managed to let myself out. Took Portia's key with me so that I could come back. You and that mutt beat me by a few minutes. And now your boyfriend has the art. *Our* art. Michael deserves that."

"Your shoes squeak, you know," I said. "I noticed it at the salon, and when you were pacing the other night."

"So what?" she said. "There are more pressing matters on my mind. Like how best to get rid of you. I'm afraid you won't topple as easily as Aaron or Portia."

"I dunno. I'm pretty tired," I said. "Walking into the police station with Aaron's femur took its toll."

She actually laughed. "I bet. And you sure beat it off the Bingham property fast. It would have been funny if it weren't so infuriating to watch the footage on my phone."

"I gather you were driving my own golf cart to take me out?"

"Missed you by minutes again. You're one lucky farmer, Ivy."

"Looks like my luck's run out." I flicked my fingers at Keats to get out of the way. "You've got me now."

"That I do." Caroline hauled back the pig poker and got ready to swing.

Over my pounding heart, I heard a steady drone. Help was on the way. Hopefully Caroline was too full of rage to hear it, too.

I dodged around the manure pile and she came after me. She was stronger and more agile than she looked, but I had pipes now, and a spade that would do the trick if it had to.

"You don't deserve to lie under a rosebush," I said, taunting her now. "I've got something more fitting in mind. Did you know manure explodes if it isn't turned regularly?"

"Did you know I'm going to kill your dog first?" she said. "Because I bet that'll hurt way more than dying yourself."

Keats ran up the manure pile and stood at the top. It was too high for Caroline to get a proper swing at him. He crouched, ready to launch, but I yelled, "Keats, no."

By this time, Caroline had started up my stairway to heaven. Keats leapt off the other side, and when she turned there was a sudden bang. And then more. Bang bang bang.

Caroline collapsed in a heap on top of the manure.

CHAPTER TWENTY-SEVEN

"**D**on't stand there gaping, you fool. Get some rope."

Edna Evans emerged from the bushes wearing camouflage fatigues. She rushed up the manure stairway and planted a boot on Caroline's chest, like a poacher with a big game kill.

"Edna, she's—"

"Unconscious. Rubber bullets, Ivy. Now get a move on it."

I started running for the truck and then remembered Kellan had sent me home with one of the female officers, whose attitude had definitely changed by that point. She checked the place out and told me to lock myself inside till Kellan arrived later. Little did he know he was sending me right into the lion's den.

Keats herded me to the barn, where I found plenty of rope. By that time, Caroline was already stirring. As I came through the back door, she sat up suddenly and grabbed Edna's boot. Edna fell backward on the manure. Keats finally had a clear shot and launched himself at Caroline. He seized her ear at the same moment a flare of orange fur arched over the pile and onto her head. She screamed and floundered in the dung, unable to get her footing to rise.

"Off, boys, off!"

I had the pig poker now but I couldn't swing while my pets or Edna were in the way. Both animals released at the same moment and bounded away. I started to swing, but Edna beat me to the punch. There was a brief, staticky sound, another scream from Caroline, and she toppled right down the mound in a heap.

Edna managed to right herself quickly but I was ahead of her with the rope. I coiled it around Caroline till she was trussed up like a Thanksgiving turkey.

"Did you just tase her?" I asked Edna, as she helped me tie off the rope.

"Sure," she said. "I have pepper spray, too."

"What about the crossbow you told me about?" I asked, shaking my head.

"Couldn't risk taking down a llama." She chuckled. "Don't think it hasn't crossed my mind, though. Nasty creatures."

"You called the cops, right?"

She tipped her head in the direction of sirens. "As soon as Red showed up in my living room window. He was howling his head off, so I got out the night goggles and saw what was happening here."

"*Percy*," I corrected. "I notice you took time to slip into your fatigues."

"You were holding your own," she said. "And I'm over eighty, in case you hadn't noticed. I need more help than a spade. But I knew I'd make good time with my new ATV. Just arrived today."

"You are something else, Edna. Seriously." I thought about hugging her and decided against it. "Thank you."

"Thank *you*," she said. "I had no idea how invigorating being a vigilante could be."

"Let's hope it's the last time," I said, as half a dozen police cars pulled in.

"Let's not," she said, with a bright smile.

I'd never seen a smile like that on her face before. She looked years younger and I finally believed her old suitor, who'd said Edna could stop a clock in her day.

"I'm going to volunteer with that Rescue Mafia," she added. "Cori Hogan and I had a chat earlier."

The first wave of cops ran around and through the barn, with Kellan and Asher in the lead. Michael Bingham was right behind them and I couldn't bear seeing the heart-broken expression on his face.

"Let's go up to the house, Edna," I said, snapping my fingers for Keats and Percy. "There's whiskey there waiting for both of us."

CHAPTER TWENTY-EIGHT

"I'm sorry," Kellan said, joining me on the porch a couple of hours later. He wanted to sit down on the swing but I kept pushing off and letting go, pushing off and letting go. Keats stayed with me and Percy was on the railing. Edna was inside by the fire with Jilly and Asher.

"Okay," I said.

"Can you stop swinging and let me sit down?"

I kept swinging. "I need the breeze in my face. I can't shake off the stink, even after two showers."

He raised his boot and stopped the swing. "Shove over, Keats."

"I need him," I said, pulling the dog closer.

"I know. But you need me, too. And I wasn't there for you in the way I should have been today. I feel terrible about what happened at the station."

"I'm sorry I embarrassed you, coming in looking like a crazy woman. Bunhead almost fainted when she realized I really am your girlfriend. Or was."

"Are," he corrected. "Even the Chief of Police makes the occasional misstep."

"You lectured me like a child in front of a dozen cops. Including my brother."

"Well, you'd put yourself in harm's way without calling me. Again." He held up his hand. "That doesn't justify a public dressing down, I admit. But you scared me, coming in with that femur, Ivy. How am I supposed to protect you if you do things like that?"

"You're not. You're supposed to protect Clover Grove while I take care of myself."

"It doesn't work like that," he said. "Even if I weren't chief it wouldn't work like that. At least for a guy like me. I need to keep my girl safe."

"I have Keats for that. And Percy."

"Is that supposed to make me feel better?"

I shook my head. "Now I have Edna, too. She is one tough old bird. It's good she has my back."

"I'm seizing the taser and the rubber bullets," he said. "She can keep the pepper spray."

"And the crossbow."

"Great," he said. "Lock up your livestock."

He kept the swing going for awhile and gradually I cooled off. Keats stayed quiet, with his muzzle in my lap, knowing his job at the moment was passive therapy.

Finally, I said, "After Keats brought me the femur, I had to run. Caroline was coming down the trail in my golf cart. Of course, I didn't know it was her at the time. I was panicking, and all I could think to do was to bring everything to you."

"It was the right thing to do in the moment," he said. "The wrong part was poking around there alone in the first place."

"I wasn't alone. And I knew Keats and Percy could find

the cameras your team couldn't. Which they did, as you know."

"I do know. And I expect you'll be reminding me of that for some time to come."

"Oh yeah." Now Keats raised his head and started a happy pant. He was sandwiched between us and while it was getting warm, I could tell he liked it. My busy dog was definitely learning to slow down and smell the fertilizer.

"Which means you're not breaking up with me," Kellan said, daring to slide his arm across the back of the swing.

"Not until you tell me what went down after I retreated with my squadron."

He sighed. "There were lots of tears. Mostly Michael's, unfortunately. As far as I can tell at the moment, he's completely innocent. I dropped him at Hazel's and they're grieving together."

"At least they have closure over Aaron," I said. "Plus they'll get a few of his treasures back."

"Michael said he's moving home and busting Hazel out of Sunny Acres."

For the first time since he joined me, I smiled. "Wonderful. I'm so happy for her. They'll have a good life together, once the stench of cat pee passes."

"Caroline also turned in her local accessory. That's who you guys were tailing through town last night. He's in custody now, too."

"So it's pretty much wrapped up."

Kellan nodded. "I always wondered about Aaron Bingham. I've been through that file over and over, and probably stood on the very place he was buried when I searched the grounds." He gingerly patted Keats' head and the dog responded by resting his muzzle on Kellan's uniformed pant leg. There were no complaints about shedding. "Well done, Keats. You deserve a medal."

I crossed my legs and let Kellan continue rocking the swing. "A medal for Keats would definitely make me forgive you. And one for Percy, too. I'd like to see their portraits lined up on the wall in your office so that Bunhead needs to see them every day. She didn't like Percy telling her off."

"Well, it was pretty loud. That's why I left my meeting. It carried right down the hall."

"Good. He likes to be heard."

"Point taken," Kellan said. "We all like to be heard. Including me."

"I do hear you. You want to protect me, and I appreciate that, I really do. But if I have ways of contributing that you don't, I want to do it. Especially when my farm, friends or family are implicated."

"So that's how it's going to be?" he asked. "You throw yourself in front of oncoming crises while I stand there wringing my hands?"

"We can work out the details," I said, snuggling in so close that Keats decided to decamp. "No hand-wringing required. Just try to be a little more patient. I'm not perfect, but I'm making progress."

He pulled me closer and kissed my forehead. "Oh, you're perfect all right. For me. Just as you are."

"Tell that to Bunhead," I said, resting my head on his shoulder. "Or wait. Let Percy do the honors."

Laughing, he kicked off again, much harder this time. For a second, I thought the whole swing-set might tip over. But it held steady under pressure, just as we had.

"I'm not selling my truck," I said. "Buttercup is too capricious."

"Fine," he said. "Can you tell me what that word means tomorrow? I just want to enjoy the peace for a bit."

Keats chased Percy across the lawn and they spun into a ball of rolling, growling, yowling fur. Down in the pasture, the donkeys started braying angrily at the disturbance. Drama Llama weighed in at the gate with indignant snorts and threats.

"So peaceful," I said, kissing Kellan on the chin. "My little slice of heaven."

CHAPTER TWENTY-NINE

"Wear the new one," Jilly said, trying to force the hanger with the pink dress I'd bought from Chez Belle into my hand. "It'll look amazing on you."

"I already know how it looks on me, remember? It's a little too tight and a lot too short."

"That's perfect! Kellan will be entranced."

"And Mom will be enraged. They call that stealing the bride's thunder."

"Oh, Dahlia will be wearing red and you know it. There's no stealing thunder from that woman." She shoved the dress at me again. "Let her roar."

"Uh-uh." I shoved the dress back at her. "How about I borrow your third best dress and see if I can ruin that, too? You can entrance my brother in this one."

She gave up. "Fine. But remember what I said about the power of the dress. And remember what Hazel Bingham says about the shortage of good men in this town."

"Kellan and I are fine, I promise. Even after that episode at the station. I don't think he'll ever live it down."

She waggled the dress. "This will help him forget."

Laughing, I retreated to my room with a black number that was fetching enough. Black felt right for the occasion of the reopening of Bloomers. It was a celebration, yes, but also a memorial. I wanted to honor Portia somehow, while acknowledging that we all had to move on.

The truck got us all there in one piece without a single stall despite my heels. Keats and Percy waltzed ahead into the salon and Mom didn't bat an eyelid. In fact, she greeted Keats like the second son she'd always wanted and Percy like a necessary evil.

To our surprise, she was also wearing black. The dress was fitted yet conservative and very flattering.

"Good find," I said, gesturing to the dress.

"It found me," she said. "When I went in to apologize to Belle Tremblay, she offered to make something special for me."

"That was gracious of both of you," I said.

"Well, we're both businesswomen, Ivy. Sometimes you have to grin and bear it." She gave me a Cheshire smile. "It gets easier when the dresses start rolling in. And Iris is going to give Belle a new cut and color next week."

There was a strange warmth in my chest as I watched her. If I didn't know better I'd say it was pride. "Nicely played, Mom."

"Thank you for all you did to clear my name and Bloomers' reputation, darling. It means a lot to me." The warmth spread from my chest to my cheeks, but then she added, "Now please, try not to be too weird tonight."

"Too weird? That's the pot calling the kettle black."

"The apple doesn't fall far from the tree, I guess. People say we're so much alike." Before I could protest, she added, "I cannot wait to introduce you to my new gentleman friend, darling. He's a dancer. So elegant." She fanned her face with her hand. "He's causing quite a stir in town."

"Which increases his appeal no end, I'm sure."

She gave me a little push. "There's Kellan. It's an honor to have such a fine-looking man in Bloomers. I'm going to offer him my classic barbershop shave... on the house."

I was quite sure Kellan wouldn't allow Mom anywhere near him with a straightedge, but I didn't ruin the mood by saying so. Instead, I went to greet him, and then we circulated for the first time as a proper couple. I didn't need to worry about Keats. He split his time between herding Kellan and shadowing Mom, which seemed like an appropriate division of labor.

There was no lasting harm done to my bond with my dog. Once I realized he didn't want to leave Caroline unsupervised at the farm with Jilly and his livestock, it explained everything. The dog carried a lot of responsibility and I would never take him for granted again.

We made the rounds to greet the guests. There were few surprises except Silvio, the bald butcher, who'd dropped his attitude after Remi found Buster in a shelter and reunited them. Turned out he also valued a classic barbershop shave.

Roy Macintosh sounded a little dubious about the straightedge, but Mom was quickly talking him down, even though Dina, his ex, was getting courted at precisely the same time by Iris. It seemed like Bloomers might stand a chance in this town after all.

Kellan and I found Hazel sitting with Percy curled up in her lap. Tears filled her eyes and she gripped my free hand tightly. "Thank you for giving my brother back to me, Ivy. And my nephew as well. We're doing better than can be expected. It turns out he's very handy and never had a chance to use his skills. Now he's buffing up the manor to its old glory. We sold one of the stacking dolls to the Langman vultures—I mean sisters—to pay for the work. Aaron would have approved of that, I'm quite sure."

"Wonderful," I said, beckoning to Edna, who hesitated in the doorway. The woman who was brave enough to tase a murderer didn't want to face the crowd of gossipmongers. I let go of Hazel's hand to try to grab Edna's but she shook me off, as I expected. "Channel your inner vigilante," I said. "You could take down anyone in an instant with your crossbow. Who else can say that?"

"No one, I hope," Kellan said. "They're illegal in Clover Grove, remember?"

"Such a stick in the mud," Edna said. "Always were from the age of five, Kellan Harper."

"Edna. He's *my* stick in the mud, thank you very much. And I wouldn't have him any other way."

"Thanks," Kellan said. "I think."

I asked Dina Macintosh to give up the seat beside Hazel so that Edna could sit down, hoping she'd rekindle an old friendship. Dina moved with such haste that I realized anew the value of having a cop for a boyfriend.

"This is great," I said, following him to a corner. The crowd opened before us as everyone stepped away from the Chief of Police. "Everyone's afraid of you so we don't have to talk to anyone."

He laughed. "Guilty consciences, probably. Everyone's got a little secret or two, don't they now?"

"And someone in this room is going to commit a crime soon," I said. "I can feel it."

"Fantastic," he said. "Well, at least it'll keep us busy."

I liked the way he said "us," as if we were now partners in crime fighting.

Leaning into him, I looked across the room to see Jilly and Asher in pretty much the same position. Tonight she'd surrendered catering fully to Mandy McCain, who was moving through the room with quiet confidence.

"For the record," Kellan said, jerking away from me suddenly, "not everyone's afraid of me."

I looked down to see Keats taking little nips at Kellan's pant legs. "Stop that. Go make sure Mom's not getting into trouble."

Mom was surrounded by men, and Keats started circling to bring them in even closer. It was a boost to both her ego and her clientele.

The place was so crowded that we tried to take up less and less space.

"When can we get out of here?" Kellan asked. "I'd rather be at the farm."

"Music to my ears, Chief." I snapped my fingers at Keats. "Play your cards right and I might let you bring in the baby goats."

"As long as it isn't the pig," he said. "Or the mean llama. I can probably handle baby goats. With Keats to help."

And with that, Kellan, Keats, Percy and I slipped out of the party and went home.

Made in the USA
Coppell, TX
14 January 2021